As they all breathed the yellow gas, and their bodies began to slow down, each had different thoughts about the upcoming excavation.

Dr. Ezekiel Bones thought: *How can there be dragons? There must be a simple explanation I've missed. If only I could see it—*

Sylvie Pharr thought: *I must remember to get him to sign the release papers* before *anything interesting happens this time—*

Reelys thought: *I should be used to space travel by now; so why does it still bother me? I should have listened to my superiors and stayed on Earth—*

Marty Szigmond thought: *She's beautiful, and she loves me—*

And Siona Jacobi thought: *Business before pleasure, old girl. Don't fall for him. You have a job to do, and jobs come first.*

Books in the Dr. Bones series:

DR. BONES™
Book 4

The Dragons of Komako

By John Gregory Betancourt

A BYRON PREISS VISUAL PUBLICATIONS, INC.
BOOK

iBooks
Habent Sua Fata Libelli

iBooks
Manhanset House
Dering Harbor, New York 11965
bricktower@aol.com • www.ibooksinc.com

Text, Illustrations, and Cover Artwork
Copyright © 1989 by Byron Preiss Visual Publications.
DR. BONES is a registered trademark of Byron Preiss Visual Publications
Developed by Byron Preiss and Paul Preuss.
Cover art by David Dorman.
Visual data by Joel Hagen.
Character design by Steranko.
Edited by Howard Zimmerman.
Series editor: Paul Preuss.
Special thanks to David M. Harris, Mary H. Higgins, Susan Allison,
and Beth Fleisher.

Library of Congress Cataloging-in-Publication Data
Betancourt, John Gregory. Dragons of Komako.
    (Dr. Bones) "A Byron Preiss Visual Publications Book."
p. cm.
    [1. Fiction—Science Fiction—Hard Science Fiction. 2. Fiction—
Science Fiction—Crime & Mystery. 3. Fiction—Science Fiction—Alien
Contact.] I. Hagen, Joel. ill. II. Title. III. Series: Dr. Bones.

ISBN 978-1-59687-949-2
January 2021

For George, Darrell, Rich, Leslie, Vince,
and everyone else at *Weird Tales*—

Thanks for putting up with me while I
wrote this one!

Table of Contents

Chapter One

Gray, mottled clouds covered the sky from zenith to horizon. They would have brought a storm on Earth, the last Knight thought as he pushed through the clumped alien grass toward the top of the hill, but here they only meant another sunless day on this godforsaken world.

He wiped the sweat from his forehead and took another sip of brandy from the plastic bottle at his belt. It would have been different if Komako were truly inhospitable, he thought. He could have dealt with the claustrophobia of underground cities, the constant sour-sweet reek of tens of thousands of close-packed human and !xaka! bodies, and the constant tension and discipline needed to work mines on airless planets. He'd been born and raised on Old Tartus, after all, and who hadn't heard horror stories of the mining operations there?

Komako's almost-but-not-quite qualities bothered him most. An oxygen atmosphere that was almost-but-not-quite pleasant to breathe, plants that were almost-but-not-quite edible. He squinted up at the sky. Even sunlight that was almost-but-not-quite there. Not that cloud cover stopped the heat from getting through.

It was hard being a Knight here. Reality kept pushing through.

Seizing a handful of the calf-high grass, he ripped it out by its roots. The damned stuff grew everywhere, finger-thick round stalks of a rubbery green, topped with clusters of grapesized black pods. It was the dominant life-form on Komako's one continent. There were no land animals above the microscopic level.

For the thousandth time the last Knight looked at the grass's roots. Dirt clung to them, but nothing else. He kept hoping he'd find a grub or an earthworm—*something* alive and moving. As he held it, the grass began to wilt in his hand, letting off a foul stink. His nose wrinkled; he threw the stalk away. Another reason there were no animals here, he thought.

The communicator at his belt chirped, but he ignored it. He'd left strict instructions that he was taking the afternoon off; his assistant could bloody well take care of anything that came up, and he'd skin the first person who bothered him, understand? They'd said they did.

He continued up the hill. When he reached the top, he paused, raising binoculars (hadn't King Arthur used binoculars?) to his eyes. A quick scan showed most of the mining operation: huge open pits to the north and west, where in his imagination great dragons lurked; offices just south of them—if you squinted, with the communications tower they became a castle. And barracks and plantation fields to the east, where his loyal peasants lived and worked.

His Komako was a rarity among mining colonies: It had good food, mainly because they could grow crops in the open. No hydroponic sludge for *his* people!

For some reason beans seemed to like Komako best of all the Earthly plants they'd cultivated, and now over a dozen different varieties grew in the plantations, along with Earth tomatoes, corn, lettuce, Sirian peppers, and other, more exotic vegetables. The only synthetics they ate were meats.

His gaze swept back to the open pits. Reality intruded again: Oddly, nothing was hazing the air over the rock-crunchers. Normally dust rose over them in suffocating clouds, as the huge machines smashed everything fed them to marble-sized bits for the smelting station. His eyes narrowed. Why would they shut down the crunchers?

"Up magnification," he said, and the binoculars obeyed. Now he could see the crunchers sitting empty, and men and robots milling about, talking among themselves, gesturing toward something he couldn't see.

"Hell's bells," he said. *Strike*, something in him said, and he had a horrible sinking sensation in the pit of his stomach. His armor was stripped away, and for the first time that afternoon he was completely Carter Simmons, planetary supervisor, head of mining operations on Beta Caloris IV—Komako, as he had christened it.

His communicator chirped at him again, incessantly this time. He snatched it from his belt, thumbing the button. "Simmons. What's going on down there? Why are the crunchers shut down?"

"Alonzo here, sir," came the too-smooth voice of his first assistant. "A problem has arisen, sir, which will require your attention."

Yes, Carter Simmons thought, it would have to be Felix Alonzo who called him: the company man's company man, a career supervisor and probably a spy for those higher up on the corporate ladder. Alonzo seemed to like delivering bad news.

"Well, what is it?" Simmons sighed. "Union troubles?" If his men were talking unions again, a few hints of what the Legion of Ares might do to support the company position would get everyone back to work. He still remembered what the Legion had done on Old Tartus the year the unions had formed and tried to strike—

"No, sir," Alonzo said. "Not unions. The latest cut in the west pit has broken into a series of what appear to be tunnels."

"So? Blast 'em and crunch the rubble, same as always."

"Sir," said Alonzo, his voice oozing smugness, "these are *tunnels*, not caves. Sentient-made. You now what that means."

Simmons pressed his eyes shut. *Not here!* This could put them months behind schedule. "Are they lona constructs?" he asked at last, daring to hope. Nobody cared about lona machines: If you avoided them, they wouldn't hurt you.

"I . . . don't think so. These are aboriginal, I would say. The men took out a couple of artifacts before anyone could stop them. Word spread, and everyone wants to see what else is there. No chance to seal it up or blast it to rubble before it's discovered—everyone knows BEC's rule about finds like this."

Simmons knew it, too: Since the Bones Energy Corporation had acquired majority control of the Panadium Trading and Mining Company the year before, new orders had been coming from the top nearly every month. One directive in particular had struck him as bizarre: If aboriginal artifacts were found, mining operations were to be suspended until a team of researchers could be dispatched from Earth. Something about a "valuable cultural heritage" and "irreplaceable alien artifacts," if he remembered correctly. It hadn't seemed terribly important at the time, but now that it applied to *his* planet. . . . Shutting down the whole mining operation just because of a few bits of alien rubbish would prove disastrous. It might be years before BEC specialists could arrive!

He chewed his lip thoughtfully. No use getting upset; there were still options left open. He hadn't gotten to the top by following rules to the letter; he'd gotten to the top by making his projects profitable. There had to be some way to turn the rules to his advantage here, or at least get around them.

Finally he said, "I'm on the hill south of the camp. Send a jumpcar to get me."

"Yes, sir!" Alonzo said.

And Carter Simmons, planetary supervisor of mining operations on Beta Caloris IV, the last Knight, eased his fifty-year-old frame down on a particularly thick patch of rubbery alien grass, leaned back, and tried to convince himself it wasn't as bad as he knew it would be.

Twenty minutes later, the jumpcar let him off in the center of the west pit. Fifty-meter-high stone walls rose hundreds of meters away on every side.

Simmons put on a hard hat, activated the servo at his belt that would warn of falling rocks, and headed for the cluster of several hundred men, women, and robots at the far end of the quarry. He was frustrated and tried to keep it from showing: A Knight was above such things, he reminded himself again and again.

Gray was the dominant color here: Dust the color of chalk coated everything, puffing up around his feet with every step. It got into your mouth and nose and left an acrid taste one almost learned to ignore.

A robot, its silver humanoid torso covered with dust, floated away from the clustered miners, calling, "Make way for the planetary supervisor! Make way!"

The gray-uniformed humans in the crowd made a corridor for him, faces peering anxiously at his as he strode past. He ignored them. Alonzo and two of the other camp supervisors—Killian, and Joe Clay—were holding an impromptu conference near the quarry wall, just in front of a huge pile of enormous boulders. Behind them, five meters up on the wall, he could see the tunnels—a pair of small, seemingly inconsequential holes roughly a meter high and twice that wide. Their ceilings curved into arches.

"There, sir," Alonzo said, pointing unnecessarily.

Simmons studied the tunnel mouths critically. "You said a couple of artifacts had been taken out?"

"Over here." Alonzo led the way to a pair of oddly shaped blue objects that had been set on a table-sized slab of rock.

Both were about waist high, with wide, tapering bases. Two thick, winglike projections jutted out at forty-five-degree angles; another, thicker projection curved up, almost like a swan's neck. But there the resemblance to statues ended: They were unmarked, smooth, and featureless.

"What are they made of?" Simmons asked, reaching out to touch one. It felt cool, hard as stone.

"Some plastic, I think, sir," said Killian, the company's explosives supervisor. He was tall and thin, with an angular face. "They're like nothing I've ever seen before."

As Simmons circled the statues, studying them from all sides, he decided they weren't birds after all—rather, they seemed dragonlike. Broad wings, chests puffed with air, head thrown back to blow gouts of fire . . . if you squinted, the base became a snakelike tail that curled around a pair of feet. Dragons were an old friend of his; he first met them in the stories his mother used to dial up at bedtime when he was a little boy. She'd loved the old tales of faery princesses and their knights in shining armor, and dragons and unicorns and all the other magical beasts had kept him company throughout the long Tartus days of his childhood. They had been the first spark to fire his imagination, and they had led to his interest in science and history. Ultimately they had motivated him to win a scholarship from the Panadium Company so he could study mining off-world.

"They're . . . *surprising*," he managed to say, after a moment's contemplation, a too-long descent into memory. "Are there more?"

"I don't know, sir," Alonzo said. "I haven't had a chance to go up and look. These two were already out when Killian notified me."

Simmons turned to the explosives supervisor.

"Wu found them," Killian said. "I sent him up with a robot to see if the next set of explosives could be detonated inside, to save drilling time. The next thing I knew, they were lugging that pair out. Wu was grinning like he'd found the mother lode, and Halani-4 started spouting off rules and regulations regarding alien artifacts . . . so I called Mr. Alonzo immediately, sir, and put off any further work until we had your say-so."

"Mmm," said Simmons. "You did the right thing. Nothing more to do here, then, until I go up and have a peek myself, to make sure it's not some hoax or freak of nature. Clear up all this"—his hand swept to cover all the rock that had fallen in front of the tunnels—"and feed it to the cruncher, and call me when it's done. We're not paying men to stand around and watch us talk."

"What do you want done, exactly?" Alonzo asked—a little too eagerly to Simmons's taste.

He wants my job. Simmons had known that for a long time, but Alonzo usually took better care in hiding his ambitions. The tunnels might well be the opportunity Alonzo had been waiting for—if Simmons misplayed the situation, he knew Alonzo would try to have him up on charges before Panadium's board of directors . . . not something to look forward to.

What would a Knight Inquisitor do?

"Should we blast the tunnels closed?" Alonzo said.

"I know the BEC rules," Simmons growled back after a moment's thought. "But even so, these bits of plastic don't mean anything until I check out the tunnels myself, and I can't check them out until there's a way cleared for me to get up there. That will be tomorrow. Till then it's business as usual. Get to it!"

That did it, got them all moving again. Clay and Killian headed for the crowd of miners, calling orders. The mining robots floated off to their tasks, and the men followed more slowly. Soon the dull roar of crunchers, bulldozers, and the other rock-moving vehicles filled the air. The ground underfoot trembled, as though living things moved just under the surface.

Satisfied, Simmons watched until everything seemed fully back to normal, then returned to his jumpcar, which still waited for him in the center of the quarry. There he paused, looking back to Alonzo as though one last thought had struck him.

"Get those, won't you?" he called, with a wave toward the statues. "Put them in my jumpcar."

"Yes, sir," Alonzo said.

"Thanks." He smiled and stepped into the passenger compartment. If Felix Alonzo wanted to play at corporate games, Felix Alonzo would certainly lose. One didn't get to be planetary supervisor on talent alone. Simmons was a Knight Inquisitor, and Knights Inquisitor have many friends. He'd never give up his power.

Behind him, he heard Alonzo barking orders. Robots with industrial grips instead of hands lifted the statues while the processors in their heads radioed instructions to the jumpcar's computer. The cargo compartment hissed open.

Simmons levered himself into his seat, tried to rub the dust from his eyes, and sighed. Those two bits of plastic were going to be nothing but headaches for him, he knew.

But now his mind had kicked into high gear, and he was turning the problem over and over. Just as suddenly as the problem had come, the answer arrived.

The rules said to shut down the mining operation. What if he just shut down the west pit? Surely that would satisfy everyone. The north pit had hit a deposit of heavy metals, and the extra miners would be useful in getting at them. He could also open up a new level there. The preliminary surveys said the metals ran deep enough. . . .

He smiled. Perhaps the tunnels wouldn't be such a disaster after all. Who knew what BEC liked? They might even *reward* him for the find.

A week later, in the grassland south of the mining camp, three men met secretly. They sat in a circle, breathing illegal stimtabs as they talked. The air over them clouded with the sweet, narcotic smoke.

"I've been thinking about these tunnels we found," said Felix Alonzo after a moment, "most especially about what's in them. It seems to be that, if BEC wants these artifact things so much, there must be a reason."

Killian cracked another stimtab and breathed deeply as a pale green mist gushed out. "Maybe they're valuable," he suggested after a moment's contemplation.

"It's worth looking into."

"I'll send one of the robots in with a holocam tomorrow and get pictures of everything," Killian offered. "I'll tell Simmons they're for his report to BEC. Our copy can go out on the next week's freighter. Our people will get it months before BEC gets any report."

"Good." Alonzo flicked open a new stimtab and sucked hungrily on it. He felt his muscles relax until his body felt like jelly, and his mind began to float. Everything became strangely clear. He said, "The organization will know what they're worth. And how to dispose of them."

"The men are curious about what's inside," Joe Clay suggested. "Whatever Simmons says or does, a few are going to try to take a peek."

"Hmm." Alonzo mulled on that for a good five minutes. Finally he decided. "We'll scare them off. Start rumors—the dragon-people are still there, bad luck comes to those who enter, etc., etc."

"Simmons won't believe that!"

Alonzo smiled nastily. "Who cares? He's not the one we need to worry about."

"What about Dmitri Wu? He's already been inside."

"Kill him." Alonzo said it without a moment's hesitation. "Make it look like an accident. 'The saurian curse,' you know."

"I know." Killian grinned. "I never liked Wu anyway."

After that, talk turned to more routine matters. Cash received from miners for the illegal drugs the three smuggled down to Camelot changed hands; plans were laid, and new shipments agreed upon.

Business was good, and looked to get better.

Chapter Two

"Dr. Bones?" asked a woman's voice.

Surprised, Zeke Bones looked up from his orange juice and said, "Yes?"

The short black woman in a military-style blue uniform standing just behind him nodded politely and reached into the pouch at her left hip. Zeke tensed a bit. The faculty club of the University of New Pennsylvania was hardly a place where people would recognize him. It might be different later that afternoon, after his guest lecture on origin myths and their relevance to archaeology, but beforehand it might well mean trouble. Plenty of people—his old enemy Bartholomew Charles heading the list—would love to see him dead.

Then he noted the Bones Energy Corporation's silver insignia on the woman's cuff. His gaze flicked to the doorway, taking in the two uniformed men with holstered handguns standing there. They were watching the whole room warily: a standard security measure for important couriers in the Bones Energy Corporation.

Zeke pushed his chair back from the table he shared with Dean Beason and Professor Moriarty. At the next table his bodyguard, Jackson Charles, sat unobtrusively munching on a breakfast roll. Jackson caught his eye and nodded imperceptibly, so Zeke relaxed. It was routine business after all, though he found the fact that BEC's courier service had managed to find him *here* a bit amazing, since he hadn't told them where he'd be today.

Scarcely a heartbeat's time had passed since the woman had come up behind him. Zeke's days at the Military Academy of Mars, and later in the Legion of Ares mercenary corps, had quickened his reaction time immeasurably. Despite his seemingly frail body, his every mental and physical faculty had been honed to precision. He often surprised those who didn't know him.

"Yes, I'm Bones," Zeke said. "Do you have something for me?"

"Yes, sir. A package from the Foundation for Exo-Cultural Preservation and Study."

Zeke knew the Foundation well. He had helped set it up to watch over BEC's numerous holdings on other worlds, and the Foundation periodically flagged information relating to alien races and sent it to him. Usually it came in the form of reports through his computer net. This was the first time they had actually sent him hard copy via a courier, and that alone was enough to pique his interest.

She offered a clipboard. "If you could sign for it, please, sir?"

"Certainly." He thumbed the box next to his name and watched as his fingerprint changed from red to green a half-second later.

"Accepted!" the clipboard chirped happily. It knew him by not only his fingerprint, but also by the unique combination of oils in his skin; it would be easy to fake one, but not both of those factors—although of course it had been done before.

"Thank you, sir," the courier said. She returned the clipboard to her pouch, then produced a small paper-wrapped package. When he took it, she turned and headed for the door. The two guards fell into step behind her.

"Something for your lecture this afternoon?" Dean Beason, head of the Art History Department, asked with interest. He leaned forward to read the package's label, but Zeke tilted it back as though reading it himself.

"No, nothing I was expecting." Zeke forced a laugh. "Routine company business, it seems—for some reason, everyone seems to want to come to me with their problems these days."

The label had read, DR. EZEKIEL BONES, PRIVATE AND CONFIDENTIAL, and bore the BEC corporate seal. Knowing it was probably quite important—and respecting the intent of its sender—he dropped it into his coat pocket before Dean Beason or Dr. Moriarty could see more. Though inside he was seething with curiosity, he knew he'd have to wait until he was alone to open it.

Dean Beason sighed sympathetically and smeared more synthabutter on his toast. "I know what you mean," he said. "My job seems just as endless."

Zeke smiled knowingly and made small talk, and soon the conversation turned to myths and morality tales. That suited Zeke; it would focus his thoughts on the coming lecture, and he would make a better speaker if his mind were entirely on the subject at hand.

Once or twice, though, he let his gaze wander across the room, settling for a second on his bodyguard at the next table. Jackson looked back, eyebrows raised questioningly. Zeke shrugged almost imperceptibly.

The mysterious package would have to wait. It wasn't every day a professor with Dr. Moriarty's reputation invited him to be a guest speaker to his anthropology class.

Later that afternoon, after an hour-long talk in a cathe-
dral-like hall packed with students and professors, came
the obligatory wine and cheese reception. Zeke found
himself surrounded by admirers.

"And you were in the Legion of Ares?" one student
asked—a blonde girl with a cherubic face. She wore a
black and purple nanosilk dress that revealed more than
it hid.

Zeke nodded. "Yes, I was. But I was much younger
then, and I hadn't decided what I wanted to do with my
life. It's certainly not a career I would recommend, if
that's what you're asking."

"No sir," she said, blushing. "I was more interested in
your travels."

He smiled encouragingly. "Ah. Actually, in a way it
was because of my time in the Legion that I became an
archaeologist. I found myself becoming more and more
interested in alien civilizations—not only those of the
lona, the shri, the !xaka!, but others as well. Did you
know that every sentient culture we've been able to com-
municate with has a number of experiences common with
mankind?"

"Like the origin myths you were talking about today?"
someone said.

Zeke nodded again, slowly. "Yes, in a way. Of course,
every alien culture has its own myths and legends. The
shri, for example, don't have anything remotely relevant
to the terrestrial Adam and Eve stories. They tell of the
Great Shri who emerged from a bolt of lightning, and
his'er offspring are all the shri of today."

So it went for the better part of three hours. The students seemed most interested in stories of his travels to
other worlds. Zeke always found ways to relate what he'd

seen and heard and done to archaeology and anthropology, and particularly to the subject of origin myths.

Then came dinner, again with Dean Beason and Dr. Moriarty, plus a bevy of the university's other important academics and hangers-on. It wasn't until seven o'clock that night that Zeke found himself finally free and winging toward his room at the New Philadelphia Hilton. With Jackson piloting the helijet, Zeke could lean back, close his eyes for a second, and relax. Although he enjoyed speaking in public, lectures always left him feeling tired and emotionally drained.

"Well?" Jackson demanded five minutes into the flight.

"Hmm?" Zeke opened one eye, knowing what his friend wanted without having to ask: He kept no secrets from Jackson Charles. They shared an almost insatiable interest in the unknown, and they'd been through so much together that they were more like brothers than employer and employee.

"I'm dying of curiosity!" Jackson said. "If you're not going to open that box they sent, give it to me and I will!"

Zeke grinned at him. "Okay, okay! I must admit I'm more than a bit curious myself. Let's take a look." He sat up and pulled the package from his pocket.

It was wrapped in plain brown paper, with only the address label to identify its source and destination. Zeke worked his thumb under the tape and worried the end open. When he turned it over, out slid a small white envelope with his name neatly hand printed on it, and a holocube.

Zeke pulled a slip of paper from its envelope and read the hastily scrawled note aloud:

BEC—Survey/Research Department
K'Kau Dshundi, Director

Zeke—

Just received this from the planetary director of mining operations on Beta Caloris IV. I thought you would want to have a look ASAP.

K'Kau

"More and more interesting," Zeke said.

Jackson murmured in agreement, programming a course into the helijet's computer and flicking on the autopilot. He stood and stretched, and muscles sleek and hard as any tiger's rippled beneath his dark, scarred skin. Most of those scars had come from his year as a paid fighter in the deathpits of his home world. His last bout had ended with his losing an eye, forcing him to retire. Through a long chain of events he'd found himself in Zeke's service. On Earth, technology was easy to get, so the latest, most realistic implant had replaced Jackson's eye. Though it had been years since he'd fought professionally, he was still incredibly fast, incredibly strong, and incredibly agile.

After he had taken a seat at the table, Zeke flicked the holocube's play button.

Instantly the air before them shimmered with a rainbow of colors, then focused into a human image. The man looked fiftyish, with a strong, clean-shaven face, graying black hair, and intense brown eyes. He was wearing a blue uniform of a cut Zeke didn't recognize, though it bore the BEC insignia in gold over the right breast pocket.

"Good day," the man said, somewhat stiffly. He seemed ill at ease talking to the holocamera. "My name is Carter Simmons. I am planetary supervisor of mining operations on Beta Caloris IV. In one of our mining pits we uncovered evidence of a now-extinct aboriginal population.

Apparently they were sentients with a low-grade technology. Per BEC's memo 2423.32.2, mining operations in that part of the quarry have been suspended. I require new instructions.

"As for what we found—there are two rooms in the quarry wall. Each one contains a few primitive artifacts. An empty tunnel extends into several other rooms, which have been unexplored as yet. The only objects of note are a pair of statues of dragons."

Here the holopic flickered uncertainly, then cut to show a small, heavily shadowed room. A beam of light darted across the wall, highlighting the sharp, angular lines of machine-made marks. The ceiling arched overhead and the walls bulged outward, as though the place had been gouged from the rock by a tunneling animal. Dozens of small grayish artifacts of every shape imaginable littered the floor. They didn't seem to be bones, or any sort of naturally occurring material. Several had sharp corners, and others had a patterned look about them that suggested their having been manufactured rather than found.

The image flickered again, and suddenly Zeke was looking at Carter Simmons once more. The planetary supervisor reached out of cameraview and lugged a statue into the picture.

The thing was dragonlike indeed, Zeke thought— almost eerily so, since no alien race *should* have known of such creatures, which existed solely in human mythology. With its serpentine arched neck, outspread wings, and small oval head, the statue seemed bizarrely unreal.

"These materials clearly have no real value," Simmons went on. "Since the aboriginals are long extinct, and their technology is so obviously inferior to ours, there is nothing to be learned from them. I would like approval to resume our regular mining schedule. Of course, if desired, we can pack up the things we found in the two rooms, plus whatever else turns up, and freighter them back to you on Earth or to one of the museums on Griynsh.*

"I await your response. Thank you for your time."

Zeke paused for a minute, deep in thought, then replayed the message, looking intently at the dragon statue and the various other artifacts. Twice he froze the holopic and examined the dragon with great attention to detail. "Impossible," he kept muttering to himself.

Finally he shut the cube off, tucked it into his pocket, and activated a servo concealed in the ring on his index finger. It was a voice-link to BEC's computer network, experimental as yet, which he was supposed to be testing whenever possible.

"Ready," the ring said.

Zeke said, "I want all the information available on the planet Beta Caloris IV, and the personnel file on Carter Simmons. Fax it to my room at the New Philadelphia Hilton."

"Compiling. Further instructions?"

"No. That's it."

"Thank you, and have a nice day."

Zeke Bones leaned back. The statues held a strange interest for him. Just today he'd used Earth's dragons as an example in his lecture, pointing out how so many different peoples in widely separated countries had myths and legends concerning them. The Chinese had them,

---

*The shri home world, where the Galactic Museum is headquartered.

the Egyptians, the Europeans . . . even native American Indians. Some researchers had even theorized that dragons were a racial memory of the dinosaurs, though little evidence existed to support such a claim. *How could aliens have them, too?*

"I know that look," Jackson said suddenly.

Zeke focussed on him. "What look?"

"That smug little smile of yours. It means we're going to go out there and have a look at that mining colony. And those statues in particular."

Zeke laughed. "You know me too well. Yes, I'm going. *Of course* I'm going! It's not every day an alien race comes up with such a close parallel to an Earth legend. I have to know why—and how."

"The dragons—?"

"Exactly."

"Don't forget your commitments here—"

"In case you've forgotten," Zeke said, "they had to cancel my classes at New Yale this semester." He touched his stomach a bit uncomfortably, remembering the series of operations they'd performed on his intestines six weeks earlier. Technically, he suffered from a virus that attacked the bacteria and enzymes in his stomach, making him unable to metabolize food. It was a recurring problem that had plagued him off and on for the last fifteen years, almost costing him his life on several occasions. Now, with a new set of genetically enhanced and—supposedly—hardier bacteria in his body, the doctors hoped his problem was permanently cured.

And, as a result of those operations, as far as the University of New Yale was concerned, he was on a sabbatical of indefinite length. His only duties for the moment were a couple of guest lectures he'd promised to deliver, and they could be cancelled with a minimum of fuss.

The autopilot beeped suddenly, and Jackson stood and went forward to land the aircar himself. Zeke glanced at his watch and did some quick calculations. It was too late to call most of the people he would want to take with him to Beta Caloris IV. Tomorrow would be soon enough. . . .

Sylvie Pharr was surrounded by whirling greens and pinks and yellows, and she didn't like it.

For reasons that escaped her she'd allowed herself to be talked into covering the latest Paris avant-garde fashions as a series of special features for a syndicated life-style show. Promises of an "award-winning woman reporter," she thought, had made potential sponsors for the program sit up and take notice.

A tall, overweight, striking blonde woman dressed in shimmering bands of green silk sauntered along the stage apron. The audience behind the floodlights *oohed* and *aahed* appropriately. The woman twirled, and four-foot-long scarves fluttered bannerlike behind her. Fat was "in" this year, and the cut of her dress accentuated her every fold and bulge.

For a second Sylvie was acutely aware of her own thinness. But life on the road either made you hard and gaunt or took you to an early grave, and she'd opted for the hard and gaunt look: It was much more practical, and what she lacked in flab she more than made up in style—the best clothes, the best makeup, the best poise. Poise was as important as talent for any reporter. And avant-garde fashions had always been "in" only among a select few.

Sylvie murmured a command word and moved her left hand, sending a holocamera coasting in behind the blonde woman. A view of the fluttering scarves would give the shot an interesting effect, if she decided to edit it into the last cut of this, the series's final segment.

It had probably been the money that made her take the job, Sylvie thought. For six ten-minute featurettes, the New Debut Show was paying about what she usually made in three months of stringing news for United Comm Interplanetary. If money had meant more, and fashion didn't bore her to death, she might have made a career of it.

Fortunately, the woman in green was the climax of the show. As the floodlights dimmed and the houselights went up, Sylvie let her attention wander. Her holocameras fluttered on the fashionable little green wings the fashion designer had made her put on them "so they won't clash with the clothes." Like a cloud of dragonflies, they settled to their customary rest positions around her feet. Their lens caps snicked into place as they stopped taping.

A runner—one of the countless indistinguishable girls who worked in fashion houses hoping for the elusive break which would put her *on* the stage instead of behind it—ran up to her.

"Vidphone, Ms. Pharr," she said, with practiced breathlessness.

"Thanks." Sylvie accepted it. After the girl had gone, she flipped back the viewscreen.

A familiar face greeted her.

"Zeke!" she said. "It's about time! I was beginning to think you'd forgotten the woman who made you famous! So what's it this time? Got an exclusive for me?"

"Whoa, girl!" Zeke Bones said. "Let's not get ahead of ourselves." He leaned back, and she could see the dark circles under his eyes. He'd obviously been up much of the night—but Zeke was like that. When something interested him, he wouldn't rest until he had it mastered. And—more important to her—his presence was almost always a guarantee of news.

"I take it this is more than just a social call?"

"Possibly," he said. "I'm going on a trip—a small vacation. I thought you might want to come."

"What sort of vacation?"

"Working. Did you ever hear of a planet named Beta Caloris IV?"

Her brow wrinkled, and she brushed her long black hair away from her face idly. "No," she said after a moment. "It's not anywhere near the Main Concourse, is it?"

"Nope. In fact, it's pushing the limits of explored space. It's basically a strip mining world, where they're raping the hell out of the land for maximum profit at maximum speed."

"Sounds thrilling."

"They've found evidence of an extinct sentient race. I'm going to make sure everything that can be preserved *will* be preserved."

"And you want me to take the pictures."

Zeke grinned. "Right."

"There's got to be something more than that. Extinct aliens are a dime a dozen."

He shrugged. "Well, perhaps a bit more. They found statues of dragons."

"So?"

"It's a bit of a puzzle, since dragons are a uniquely human concept. Perhaps it's a bizarre coincidence, or perhaps they're a hoax of some kind. Whatever, they've got my interest, and since I'm not teaching this semester, I'm going. Are you up for an extended trip?"

"How long?"

"At least two months. If things work out, possibly longer."

"I'll have to check my schedule," she said, trying not to sound *too* eager, and knowing she'd come along no matter what her schedule said.

"Great! I'll reserve your seat on the *Ostrom*. Can you catch a shuttle and meet us in orbit tomorrow?"

"Mmm . . . I think I can manage it. I have a bit of editing to finish up first, plus a stand-up and a couple of voice-overs. Where are you now?"

"New Philadelphia Hilton."

"If I finish tonight, I might even be able to catch a red-eye flight and see you in New Philadelphia tomorrow."

"I'll expect you at the shuttleport, then. Oh, and Marty says hello."

Sylvie snapped upright. "You didn't say that little gnome was coming—"

But the vidphone had bleeped and was already growing dark. Zeke Bones had hung up.

The shri Reelys hovered over the computer table, uncoiled tentacles dangling motionlessly like a tangle of cut-off garden hose, his'er blue mantle unfurled, eyestalks twisted to focus on the display screen directly beneath his'erself. Interesting things were happening with Dr. Ezekiel Bones, if the computer were to be believed. Reelys couldn't tell exactly *what* information Zeke had accessed, but s/he could tell the quantity—and from the amount of raw data Zeke now had sitting in his computers, he was up to something big.

Since Reelys had accepted a consulate job at the shri embassy on Earth, s/he had had plenty of chance to carry out his'er latest assigned task: spying for the shri government. For the shri "spying" mostly meant keeping tabs on humans in whom the shri had an interest—and Reelys had made Bones a special project.

Ever since they'd served in the Legion of Ares together Reelys had been involved with that most amazing human. As chief medical officer on the Legion ship upon which they both had served, Reelys had patched Zeke up countless times after battles, and even performed the first half-dozen stomach operations that had kept Zeke alive when his body began failing him.

Yes, if something were happening, Reelys certainly wanted to know about it. S/he let his'er tentacles coil a bit, and by jetting a slight stream of air from his'er gasbag, propelled his'erself toward the far wall. A touch of a tentacle and the shri embassy's pool of vehicles dispatched a helijet for him'er.

A visit to Bones seemed most appropriate.

Marty Szigmond squawked like a wounded parakeet when he heard the news.

"What do you *mean* it's a whim?" he said. "As if I don't have better things to do than go chasing all over the universe on whims!"

"Sylvie Pharr has agreed to come."

"That damned busybody—"

"And Jackson, too."

"What do you need *that* lazy lump for? I can do anything he can, and ten times better!"

"It's more of a vacation than anything else."

"Next you'll be telling me that stinking dung-beetle is coming with us."

"Actually, Kadak!xa is off-world right now. I couldn't get in touch with her. But if you want I could try—"

"Futz!" Marty threw up his hands and stomped from the room, making agonized faces and gagging noises.

Zeke struggled to keep a straight face, and failed. Marty Szigmond was, at 4'3", far from an imposing figure. Short, fat, and bald, his silver skin and black eyes with white pupils made him seem more the product of some demented cartoonist than anything else. He was hlidskji—from Tau Ceti 4, one of the first planets colonized by Earth—and the colony's robot geneticists had altered his race's stock until it fit the planet as though it had evolved there. His occasional outbursts were something Zeke had learned to live with.

After a minute, when it looked like Marty wasn't coming back in a hurry, Zeke followed him into the suite's sitting room. Marty was sprawled across the sofa, arms crossed, looking angry.

"There's something wrong, isn't there?" Zeke said softly. "You're not acting like yourself."

"A lot you'd know about it! No sooner do I meet her—the most beautiful woman ever to grace this miserable old planet of yours—when you start conspiring to tear us apart!"

"Oh?" Zeke's eyebrows shot up in surprise. "Who is she?"

Marty sighed deeply, and a dreamy look came over his face. "A goddess!"

"Hah!" said Jackson, from the doorway of his room. He had a suitcase in each hand—already packed for the shuttle that afternoon. "More likely a silver tire from some land truck. More your speed, right, Marty?"

"Stop it already!" Zeke said, before Marty could answer. "You're giving me a headache. If you want to, Marty, you're more than welcome to stay on Earth—"

"You'd be lost without me, and you know it!"

"—or you could ask this goddess of yours along for the trip. This is supposed to be a vacation, remember, and that doesn't preclude having fun."

Marty grinned, showing silver teeth, and leaped from the sofa. "Terrific, boss! I'll let her know."

He rushed from the room, and as he passed Jackson he somehow managed to stomp on both of the big man's feet.

Yelping, Jackson dropped his suitcases beside the others at the door and limped to the sofa. "I guess I deserved that," he muttered, settling down and kicking off his shoes. He rubbed his toes ruefully. "But sometimes he just rubs me the wrong way."

"I know, I know," Zeke said. "And you just couldn't resist."

The vidphone rang before Jackson could reply. Zeke crossed to the desk and tabbed the answer button. The vidscreen flickered to life.

"Good morning, Dr. Bones," said one of the hotel's receptionists. "There is a shri here to see you. It says it doesn't have an appointment, but that you know it. Do you want it shown up to your suite?"

"What's his'er name?" Zeke asked.

"A moment, sir." The man bent out of view, asked something, and quite distinctly Zeke heard the shri's whistled answer: "Reelys."

"Show him'er up," Zeke said. Then he flicked off the vidphone and swiveled the chair around to face Jackson once more.

"It seems," his bodyguard said, "our party's growing by the minute."

• • •

When Zeke opened the door for Reelys, he found the shri had folded his'er mantle and stood, delicately balanced, on his'er mass of green tentacles. With his'er airbag deflated, Reelys's body looked for all the world like a translucent cylinder. As s/he moved into the room, s/he unfolded his'er mantle and began inflating his'erself to a more normal size.

"Good morning," Zeke said. "I tried to reach you earlier today, but the embassy staff said you had gone out for the afternoon."

"Indeed," said the shri, voice a soft hiss. "I had a feeling you might want to see me, and so I decided to stop here and speak to you."

Jackson said, "Even if I believed in coincidences, which I don't, that would still be a very weak explanation."

"It is the only one I have."

"It doesn't matter," Zeke said. "I'm glad you're here, Reelys. We're leaving for Beta Caloris IV tomorrow—for a small working vacation." Quickly he explained the situation, and Reelys's mantle darkened slightly when he mentioned the dragon statues.

"Very curious indeed," the shri said. "In my readings of your great works of literature, I have often found references to dragons. It is a fascinating coincidence. I would be delighted to accompany you and lend you whatever assistance I can . . . if you are sure you do not mind my presence?"

"Actually," Jackson said, "coincidences aside, I'll be glad you're there. Zeke's been having trouble with his stomach again, and I'd be more comfortable with a doctor along. You can fix him up if anything goes wrong."

"What sort of trouble?" Reelys hissed. "Why was I not consulted? I've spent more time inside your body than any human surgeon."

"Routine bacteria replacement," Zeke said. "But then you knew that. You access *all* my medical records often enough, according to BEC's security department."

The shri seemed to shrink a bit. "Am I that obvious?"
"Yes."

Jackson looked from one to the other, puzzled. "What do you mean?"

Zeke winked. "Let's just say Reelys has been keeping tabs on me, and that's why s/he's here." He looked at the shri. "I assume you came prepared to leave with us?"

"Of course."

"Terrific." He looked around and, not seeing Marty, shouted, "We're leaving now. Do you want to come with us, or meet us at the shuttle?"

Marty called back, "At the shuttle!"

Zeke surveyed the room one final time. He couldn't think of anything he'd forgotten. "I guess that's it," he said, and started for the door. Reelys and Jackson fell in step behind him.

Chapter Three

Noon on Komako was the worst part of the day, Carter Simmons thought. The air 'freshers in his office couldn't keep up with the humidity, or the heat, or much of anything. They had been designed for subterranean mining conditions, where the biggest problem was keeping the stink of the mines and the miners out of the corporate headquarters. Now his office felt more like a sauna than anything else; not even his knighthood fantasies could bring escape.

He took a sip from his plastic snifter of brandy and wiped the sweat from his forehead. This was his third drink that morning—privilege of rank, and all that—so when a knock came at his door, he was feeling less terrible than usual.

He shouted, "Come!" and actually managed an almost cheerful tone.

Felix Alonzo slipped in, looking dutifully concerned. Annoyingly, Simmons noticed, Alonzo's uniform appeared neat and crisply pressed—not a hint of sweat. Somehow the bastard always managed to be the consummate mining professional. Simmons looked like hell at the moment, rumpled and sweaty, and he wished more than anything in the universe that Alonzo looked that way, too. It would have made talking to him infinitely easier.

Instead of complaining about it, though, he waved Alonzo toward the formchair in front of the desk, sloshing brandy from the snifter as he did. As the brandy pooled on his plastic desktop, he mopped at it with a memo pad, making things worse.

"Sir," said Alonzo, after a minute of this had gone by.

"Yes?" Simmons asked. He looked around for something to set the dripping memo pad down on, and finally put it on the base of the artificial fern potted behind him. "What brings you this time? More bad news?"

"I'm afraid so, sir. This morning's blasting opened up still more aboriginal tunnels."

"Where?"

"Level 34, north pit."

It was definitely growing hotter in the office. Simmons mopped at his forehead. That afternoon, he swore, he'd have the technicians in to look at his 'fresher, to see if anything could be done.

"That's the sixth group this month, isn't it?" he finally said, taking the opportunity to refill his drink. Pointedly, he didn't offer any to Alonzo. *Hate that man*, he thought.

"Yes, sir." Alonzo shifted foot-to-foot, looking a trifle disturbed.

"Anything in them this time?"

"No, sir. Just the usual small odds and ends—enough to shut down that level of the pit, certainly, per BEC's instructions."

"Any more of the dragon statues?"

"No, sir. Not a one."

Simmons sighed, and his brow wrinkled as he thought. If it hadn't been for BEC's directives. . . .

In the six months since he'd sent that first report to his superiors at BEC, his men had found seventeen more tunnels. It would have been all right if they'd been in one small area; then he could've just shifted operations and kept going at the same pace. Instead, though, the aliens had built everywhere—test pits north, west, even south of his camp had found tunnels, and in them traces of the aliens' civilization. Fortunately they were always at deep levels—he'd been having his crews keep to newer, shallower pits as much as possible for the last couple of months, and as a result mining operations had gone relatively smoothly. Still, his men turned up a couple of the tunnels every few weeks, and each time he'd made out yet *another* report in triplicate, and earmarked it for his superiors' attention at BEC. And then he'd shut down that part of the operation and started a new pit in a new location.

And as if BEC's directives didn't present enough problems by themselves, he'd been having trouble with his miners, too. The superstitious louts all thought the saurians were still in the tunnels, hiding. They'd rather blame an accident on a mythical alien than admit to their own carelessness on the job.

It would've been so much easier if he could just blast the tunnels and everything inside them once and for all. He nodded to himself.

Damn aliens. They'd probably built their tunnels just to inconvenience him. And those idiots at BEC who'd come up with the regulations regarding aboriginal aliens and their civilizations—if he ever cornered them in a dark alley with a lasergun—

Alonzo cleared his throat.

Simmons glared up at him and said, "You ordered all operations there shut down, I suppose."

"Yes, sir. I've also stopped blasting in that sector, pending your approval. And, of course, you'll want to inspect the new tunnels yourself, to verify that they're indeed of aboriginal origin—"

"Yes, yes," Simmons said, waving one hand vaguely. He remembered not to spill his brandy this time. "I'll look into it first chance I get. Priority assignments first—I have all these progress reports to finish up, since they must go out with the next shuttle, and then I need to recheck the final figures for this quarter's operations. And *then* there's the payroll. . . ."

"Yes, sir." Alonzo nodded, wheeled around, and marched from the room as straight-backed as any soldier ever was.

Carter Simmons watched the door close, then drained his snifter and hurled it after Alonzo. It bounced off the synthawood with a pleasant *thunk.*

Carter Simmons didn't feel at all like a Knight Inquisitor today.

Late that evening, as the miners below counted evening, the Poseidon-class freighter *Constellation* lumbered into orbit around Beta Caloris IV. She was a huge starship, one of the largest in the Panadium Mining Company's fleet, and her sixteen holds would each carry fifteen hundred metric tons of cargo. From a distance, she resembled a string of gigantic metal cubes: Each cargo hold was a gigantic box, linked one to another by electromagnetic couplings. Shuttles would lift cargo to orbit, and from there the *Constellation*'s robodrones would shunt it into her holds.

She took readings from the dozen-odd satellite beacons orbiting Beta Caloris IV and moved to a position just over the mining camp on the planet's one continent.

Beta Caloris IV was dark below, but the oceans had a distinct phosphorescence, and the land mass stood out in silhouette.

From the silver sphere at the front of the *Constellation*—the command station, where the freighter's pilot and crew lived—the primary shuttle glided from its berth. Thrusters flared for half a second, and the shuttle rolled to the left, upside down in relation to the *Constellation*. Burnished silver in color, shaped like a cigar with wings, it slid across the planet like a giant bird. Its thrusters fired once and it started the long fall down.

Ten minutes later, as it hit atmosphere, its hull began to glow orange, then white. A contrail tens of meters long flared behind it, marking its passage. It screamed across the sky.

Below, scattered miners came out from the company cantina to watch and cheer and raise their mugs in salute—they knew the routine. First the pilot came down for the paper work, and if it all checked out (which it had better), the next day he'd bring down the starship's cargo: mail from friends and family on other worlds, the latest news and entertainment vids, taped magazines and books, more food and drink to stock the company stores—everything that made life bearable on a frontier mining world.

Three kilometers up, the shuttle finished its first stage of braking. Now it moved at a manageable velocity, just below the speed of sound. Its pilot took a long, slow banked turn and headed for the duracrete runway north of the camp. Floodlights flicked on there, as guidance computers took over the shuttle's navigation.

As it roared overhead, a scant fifteen hundred meters above Carter Simmons's house, the Knight Inquisitor stirred uneasily in his dreams.

Felix Alonzo was the only one out at the runway that night to greet the *Constellation*'s shuttle pilot. As the little craft touched down on the runway, wheels squealing, its engines reversed thrust with a roar.

When it had slowed to a crawl, its pilot nosed the shuttle around and taxied it toward the warehouses, where Alonzo stood waiting. The mining supervisor touched the miniature microphone at his throat.

"Any trouble?"

Static hissed, then came: "No."

"You're two days off schedule," he said.

"The *Constellation* had a wee bit of engine trouble leaving Karma Station, but it wasn't anything we couldn't handle. How's business?"

"Good and bad. Come on out and we'll talk."

The shuttle finally stopped. In the sudden silence that followed the engines shutting down, Alonzo could hear the ship making little clicking noises, like a geiger counter, as its metal cooled and contracted. The sharp smell of ozone filled the air.

Then the side hatch popped open, a ramp extended, and the familiar form of the pilot emerged: Bill Wagner, a tall, broad-chested man, his dark hair long and lank, his beard thick and greasy looking. He carried a huge duffle bag slung over one shoulder. For a second he paused, squinting into the floodlights and breathing deeply. Then he headed for the ground with a swagger.

The man's smell hit Alonzo first—putrid, like canned meat gone bad. That's what all spaceships stank like, from the close press of unwashed bodies, from the recycled air, from the recycled hydroponic sludge all spacers had to eat. A man who stayed aboard a spaceship started to smell that way, too, after a time.

As Wagner drew close, Alonzo gagged a bit, and covered his mouth and nose with a handkerchief.

"Good to see you, too, Felix," Wagner said loudly, seizing Alonzo's free hand in a powerful grasp and pumping it long and hard.

Alonzo disentangled himself as quickly as he could. "Same goes for me, Bill," he said through the handkerchief. "Got anything special for us this time?"

He laughed. "Cuttin' right to business, eh? Don't be so impatient—there're more important things than makin' money. I sure could use a bath, I bet, from the pretty way you're turnin' green."

"I couldn't agree more."

Bill took in a deep breath of air and thumped his massive chest. "Ah, that planet air! Nothin's sweeter! You groundirts don't know how lucky you are!"

"Your sense of smell's dead," Alonzo said. "The air here's horrible."

Bill giggled, almost like a child. "You try makin' a two-year run through the minin' colonies and see if it don't change your tastes a bit! Now, you want me to splash some water over myself, or no?"

"You know there's a shower in the guest house," Alonzo said, turning to lead the way. "You've been here often enough. Come on, I'll get you settled in."

Bill giggled again and caught Alonzo's arm. "I reckon I know the way, all right. But first, I got a message here for you, right from the boss himself." He reached into his pocket, pulled out a datachip, and flipped it to Alonzo.

Alonzo caught it and slipped it in his right shirt pocket. He'd view it later, when he was alone. Not that Wagner hadn't already seen it: Space travel took a long time, and people got awfully bored along the way. Alonzo would have viewed the chip himself, if he'd been sent to deliver it. Knowledge gave you power, and he'd always been big on power.

"Now," Bill said, starting for the guest house, "what's this about business being good and bad?"

And Alonzo spent the next ten minutes telling him how the latest series of tunnels had shut mining operations down to a quarter of their normal efficiency.

A twenty-minute walk brought them to the guest house. It sprawled; there was no other way to describe it. Starship pilots had always gotten all the comforts the Panadium Trading and Mining Company had to offer, and on Camelot it was no different.

For a long moment Bill Wagner merely stood in the doorway, studying the intricate geometric sculptures on the walls, the plush gray carpets on the floors which hid the gray dust, the decadently soft sofas and chairs. Nothing had changed since he'd last been here. The main room still resembled a meeting hall in size and shape; over fifty people could have comfortably gathered there.

"It'll do," Wagner said, moving forward.

Alonzo followed him in. A robot butler floated over to them, looking somewhat comical in its black tie, tuxedo shirt, and tails.

It said, "May I take your bag, sir?"

Wagner handed it over. "I'm going to take a long hot bath first thing," he said. "Lay out clothes for me."

"Immediately, sir," it said.

"Sterilize them first," Alonzo said quickly.

"Of course, sir." It turned and headed for the bedroom.

Alonzo took another envious glance around the room. Not even Carter Simmons lived so well, he thought. Not that he would've traded places with Wagner. But when he retired form the mining company, he wanted a house like this—

Wagner stretched luxuriously and began untabbing his shirt. "See you in an hour," he said. He wandered into the bedroom after the robot.

Alonzo went outside to wait. Away from the runway's floodlights, it was as dark as he'd ever seen it before. Overhead, the clouds had parted for the first time in weeks, revealing the glories of the universe. The stars were close together here, and they lit the sky like nothing he'd ever seen before, a stardust trail spanning the length of the heavens like a spilled cup of wine.

He sat with his back against the guest house's wall. A soft wind blew, ruffling his hair. When he closed his eyes he could imagine himself on Earth, living the life he'd always dreamed of. . . .

Finally he knew he had to get down to business. Just as he'd never been one to pass up a chance for more power, Felix Alonzo had never been one to pass up easy money. It was a weakness of his character. He recognized that weakness, and had always been careful never to let it get the better of him. He was a company man first, and only second a smuggler. Forced to choose between the two, he would have stayed with the company because of the security it offered—a pension in his old age, full medical benefits, a chance for increasing power and prestige as he rose in the company's ranks.

When he'd been young and naïve, he'd planned to spend his entire life serving the Panadium Mining Company. Now he planned to serve it until his private, numbered bank account had more money than he'd ever be able to spend in his entire lifetime. He figured he had five more years as a smuggler before he'd be able to retire.

Pulling the datachip from his pocket, he sat with his back to the guest house, snapped the chip into his belt computer, and tabbed it on.

The vidiscreen flickered to life. Whoever had recorded the message had used a face/voice scrambler. He saw a figure of indeterminate sex sitting in near-darkness, and the person's features shifted every few seconds, nose growing and shrinking, lips moving in all directions, eyes yellow and squinty, then blue and large, then black like a hlidsjki's. The person's hair changed, too: first black, then red, then silver, then green. Even the clothing shifted color and style every few seconds.

When the man—Alonzo assumed it was a man—spoke, it was in a weirdly warbling voice that made Alonzo's skin crawl.

"The artifacts have interested us," he said. "There is a small market for such items—there are always a few collectors who appreciate such things, and wish to possess them privately as part of an art collection with no questions asked. We have shown your holos to a number of dealers in such goods, and they in turn showed them to their customers. A few have already made inquiries about the statues and other items. We will take however many you can obtain. Pack them for vacuum conditions, and send them out as part of the next ore shipment. The usual pay and bonuses will follow. End."

The vidiscreen blanked.

Alonzo found himself breathing more quickly. He'd been right—there were collectors interested in alien artifacts. It would be easy . . . almost too easy . . . to ship off the statues. The bonuses might even put him ahead in his retirement plans.

For the last six months, in anticipation of the go-ahead from his bosses, he'd been stockpiling the dragon statues and every other interesting Camelotian artifact he could find. Now he had literally hundreds of artifacts stashed with the main supply of stimtabs and other, harder drugs his men supplied to the miners.

He smiled. *It's almost too easy.* Being camp supervisor meant he went into the tunnels ahead of everyone else— to make sure they were of aboriginal origin, of course— and that also meant he got first look at and first pick of all the alien goodies. Less than a quarter of what he found ever made it into that drunken slob Simmons's reports.

Now, with the go-ahead, he'd have to start packing everything up. It would mean some extra-long nights for him and his men, but it would be worth it. Yes, things were certainly looking up.

He smiled.

Not long after that, Bill Wagner strolled out from the guest house, toweling his hair dry. He'd changed to a clean black uniform, but the pungent smell of decay still clung to him. *Probably in his hair and skin,* Alonzo thought, forcing a smile. *Probably in every fiber of his body. Probably never come out.* At least it was tolerable now, though, masked by soap and cologne from the guest house's stores.

"Let's go see your boss," Wagner said.

Alonzo got to his feet. "It's rather late. He'll be drunk, or asleep. Probably both."

"So? It'll be easier to make my report that way. More fun, too." He giggled. "Lots more fun!"

Alonzo smiled, for real this time. "I can't wait."

They headed for Simmons's house.

Chapter Four

Zeke was already strapped into the pilot's seat of the *Ostrom*'s shuttle, the *Heinrich Schliemann*, running last-minute checks before departure, when the pair of yellow taxis pulled up in front of the ship almost simultaneously.

He put down his clipboard and watched the monitors with interest as Sylvie Pharr climbed out of the first taxi, retrieved her credit card from the robot driver, and headed for the shuttle's on-ramp. Around her, various holocams hovered. She stopped ten meters from the shuttle and, as the cameras photographed her with the *Heinrich Schliemann* in the background, raised a microphone and began a stand-up report of some kind.

Zeke sighed. She'd probably talked some educational company into letting her do a documentary on the legendary (soon-to-be, anyway) Dragon Statues of Beta Caloris IV. She was hard to resist under any circumstances, and if she were trying to hard sell someone something—good luck to him getting away without it! Still, he couldn't blame her; she lived for her job. Though he'd hoped to put that behind them this trip, to get to know the real woman behind the tough reporter façade.

He turned his attention to the other taxi. Marty Szigmond was already standing on the ground, stretching.

As Zeke watched, the hlidskji reached up to the shuttle door and helped someone else out.

She was short, fat, bald, and her skin was the color of aluminum foil.

In fact, Marty's goddess looked exactly like a female version of Marty. She even had the same bizarre taste in clothes: She wore a shocking purple dress, matching lipstick, and a squarish purple hat. Against her silver skin, the effect was startling. *Just so she doesn't have Marty's personality*, Zeke thought. One Marty was often as much as he could take.

A light flashed on the control panel. He ticked that check off the clipboard, fed the mass notation into the autopilot, and then decided the shuttle was ready.

"Get me Flight Control," he said to the computer.

"Yes, Captain Bones."

A second later the vidiscreen flicked on and a woman's face appeared. "FC 221, Cynthia speaking. What can I do for you, *Heinrich Schliemann?*"

"All systems have checked out now. I'd like to schedule a launch window, please."

"Just a sec . . ." She did something at the keyboard in front of her. "Next opening in half an hour. Three-twenty for the one after that."

"Half an hour's a bit close, but we can manage it."

"Good. I'll slot you in. Switch control over to me now, please."

"Right, and thanks."

She grinned. "Always a pleasure, Dr. Bones." Then she switched off.

"Jackson!" Zeke called as he keyed in the acceptance which would turn the shuttle's controls over to the computers at Flight Control.

A moment later his bodyguard poked his head into the pilot's cabin. "Yeah, boss?"

"Why don't you help Marty get his guest aboard, and get whatever luggage they have stowed away. There's a launch window opening for us in half an hour, and I'd like to take it now that everyone's here. It'll get us up to the *Ostrom* hours ahead of the schedule we projected."

"Sure thing, boss." He ducked out.

Zeke made sure Flight Control's computer had actually come on-line, then unstrapped himself and stood, taking one last lingering survey of the controls. All the proper lights glowed green: fuel tanks full, computer self-diagnostics passed, everything checked out.

Finally satisfied, he went to see about Sylvie and the two hlidskji.

The passenger cabin was a zoo.

Reelys had completely deflated his'er airbag and now sat in an acceleration couch, folded mantle looking like a deflated beach ball. Sylvie Pharr stood interviewing the shri, cameras whirring and buzzing about them on func-tionless little pink wings.

"—which leads us to our expedition's leader, Dr. Ezekiel Bones," Sylvie was saying. "You've been with him a long time, haven't you, Reelys?"

"Certainly," the shri whistled back. "Ezekiel and I served together in the Legion of Ares. You might say we helped each other explore our mutual interests in alien artifacts. I remember once, on Pavo 6—"

Beyond them, Jackson was stowing baggage into the rear cargo compartment, while Marty supervised him—or tried to.

"I know how to tie down luggage, runt!" Jackson finally bellowed.

Marty's girlfriend clung to Marty's arm. She stared at Jackson Charles haughtily, and in a sharp voice said, "Yes, I'm sure you can do a perfectly passable job. But if you want to get it done *absolutely* right, you had better listen to Marty. He's *so* smart about such things. You could learn a lot from him."

Jackson turned his back on them, grumbling to himself. Zeke could read the frustration in the tenseness of his back and shoulders.

Smiling to himself, Zeke raised his hands. It took a few seconds, but soon everyone had turned and was looking at him expectantly. Sylvie sent her cameras zooming over to surround him, and their lenses whirred as they focussed on his face.

"Are these things really necessary?" Zeke asked her. "This was supposed to be a vacation."

"I've got to pay my bills, Doc. You understand. Besides, you're the most famous archaeologist in the galaxy, and you can't let your public down!"

Zeke cleared his throat and frowned, not liking the sound of that. Publicity had gotten in his way in the past, and he wouldn't have gladly suffered this trip without the promise of still more to come. He finally said, "Takeoff is in about twenty minutes, so we just have time for a quick round of introductions. Marty, would you care to do the honors?"

Marty swaggered to the center of the cabin, pulling his goddess along with him. All eyes focused on her. "Everyone, this is Siona Jacobi, my heart of hearts, my flame of flames—the one and only true love of my life!"

Quickly he introduced Siona to everyone.

"I'm delighted to meet you," Zeke said.

Siona practically cooed. "When Marty told me you'd invited me along on your dig, I was *sooo* excited!" she said. "I watch you *all* the time on the newsvids!"

"Any friend of Marty's," Zeke said. "Really, I'm happy you could come. You're sure you won't be missed? We'll be gone for several months, you know, and it seems like you're going on very short notice—"

"Natch," said Siona. "I was just visiting Earth—sort of being a tourist, you know?—when I met Marty here." She pinched his cheek and Marty's face darkened noticeably. "I was supposed to be touring the Americas for the next six months, but loverboy swept me off my feet. Isn't he gorgeous?"

Marty looked away. "Aw, Siona—"

"Snookums . . ."

As they mooned over each other, Sylvie caught Zeke's eye and mimed gagging. Zeke grinned at her and shrugged. "Each to his own tastes," he whispered. "She suits him."

Zeke crossed to Reelys and bent to check the shri's acceleration harness. "How are *you* doing, pal?"

"Fairly well so far, Zeke. Leaving a planet is really the hardest part—we shri are not built for this sort of bodily stress, you know."

Zeke knew; the shri were built for floating through delicate crystalline cities in the clouds, rather than life on land. Even their starships, with their huge molecule-thin sails spread kilometers wide to catch the solar winds, were things designed for a more placid existence.

He said, "Just wait till we get to the *Ostrom.*"

"The next thing you know," Sylvie told him'er, "we'll be in orbit around Beta Caloris IV."

"That is the one nice thing about the *Ostrom.* I hate travel by regular human starships."

"You're just spoiled," Zeke said. "But then, so am I, so I shouldn't complain."

He checked the time, then turned to Sylvie. "We lift off in five minutes. Want to watch from the pilot's cabin? Quite a view."

"I'd love to," she said.

"Just leave the cameras in here. There's no room for them up front."

By the time the shuttle neared the *Ostrom* in orbit four hours later, Zeke was starting to have second thoughts about having asked Siona along. She wasn't obnoxious in any way—she just had a cloying sweetness about her, and seemed to have infected Marty with it, too. They stayed in the back of the shuttle, talking quietly, giggling every now and then, and once in a while kissing.

"Where did he find her?" Sylvie asked. Now that her holocams were off and stowed away, she seemed almost a different person—a friend rather than a reporter pressing for answers. It had been a long time since Zeke had seen her this way . . . too long, he thought.

"I don't know," he said. "The first I heard about her was this morning, when I told Marty I was planning a trip. Then suddenly he started pouting, and the next thing I knew, I'd invited her along, too."

"Mmm." Sylvie glanced back at the two of them. They were too engrossed in their own conversation to notice they had become the subject of discussion at the front of the shuttle. "She seems almost *too* perfect for him for my tastes."

Zeke raised his eyebrows. "Why, I do believe you're jealous!"

"Of *her*? Come on, Zeke, give me *some* credit for taste. I'd sooner have Reelys here for a boyfriend than Marty."

"Why, thank you," the shri said, the blue of his'er mantle darkening slightly. His'er tentacles writhed with pleasure. "I would sooner have you for a mate than Marty, too. Not that I have any dislike for Marty, of course—he's a perfectly wonderful fellow."

"Of course," Sylvie said hastily. "It's all a matter of degree. What I'm talking about is a bad feeling I have about her. I guess you could call it intuition—or a premonition."

The autopilot chimed softly. "That's my call," Zeke said. "Ready to watch the docking?" he asked.

"Sure!"

The *Ostrom*, originally christened the *Ogilvie T. MacPherson*, was one of the earliest ships to be equipped with the then-experimental invariance overdrive. From stem to stem she currently measured seventy-two meters, which included all the latest in microwave relay dishes, satellite tracking systems, navigation beacons, and radio directional antennae. From space, she looked like a long silver box whose sides bristled with silver rods.

Zeke's father had originally outfitted the *MacPherson* as a survey and prospecting ship, with extensive laboratories, exploration equipment, storage bays for fuel and mineral samples, and quarters to keep a good-sized crew in comfort for long periods of wakefulness. When Zeke took over, though, he had refurbished the labs, augmented the prospecting tools with instruments for excavation and recovery, and converted the storage bins to biostats for preservation of living samples. The addition of a much larger computer, a complete library, and video editing facilities completed the major improvements.

Zeke then rechristened the ship in honor of the Old Yale scholar John Ostrom, a twentieth-century paleontologist who had championed the theory of "hot-blooded" dinosaurs. The *Ostrom*'s two shuttles he had

named the *Heinrich Schliemann*, after the German archaeologist who had discovered the fabled lost city of Troy,
and the *Lord Caernarvon*, after the English nobleman who
had supervised the excavation of King Tut's tomb.

All things considered, the *Ostrom* was, in many ways,
the best ship in human space . . . certainly she was the
finest in terms of comfort for crew and passengers. It was
all because of the invariance overdrive, which BEC
researchers had developed as an alternative to time-
consuming travel through black hole stations.

Invariance overdrive was a deliberate, controlled
annihilation and reanimation of the ship, deriving energy
from the antimatter fuel component. The transition
could be performed at any stage of the journey, but was
safe only near the end, when all variables could be spec-
ified accurately.

During the annihilation process, the charge, parity,
and time of every particle of the ship were reversed; total
charge was conserved, total parity reversed and
re-reversed, the time sign reversed, and its quantitative
value reset before being re-reversed. A ship emerged from
a successful invariance transition with the same position
and momentum in space, but with an adjusted *relative*
time value. Which is to say, the ship had in fact travelled
the entire distance, but its timeline had been distorted so
that it appeared, in realtime, to have made the trip
instantaneously.

The only real problems with invariance overdrive
were its great cost—antimatter didn't exactly grow on
trees—and the fact that the annihilation-reanimation
process wasn't entirely efficient. Since on average one
part in five trillion of the mass of the ship—including
passengers—failed to make the transition, there was

always some physical damage to both the *Ostrom* and its crew. Usually it was minor enough to pass completely unnoticed.

It was a simple matter to leave Earth orbit, calculate the course to Beta Caloris using pulsars as coordinate-beacons, and begin a comfortable one-gee acceleration. The ship would keep going through the aeons, accelerating until it neared the speed of light, then make an invariance transition when it neared its destination.

Once the course was set and the computers took over, nothing remained for the humans to do. The *Ostrom* was capable of running on complete automation, and her computer could better navigate the course than any pilot.

Zeke brought everyone to the center of the ship, to the hibernation chambers. They radiated out from the center of the room like the spokes of a wheel, each cylinder resembling a silver coffin more than anything else. The transparent flexiglass tops had all been swung back, and the jelly-cushioned interiors gaped invitingly.

"Do we really have to sleep the whole way?" Siona asked.

Zeke nodded. "You won't miss a thing," he said. "You'd be several thousand years old by the time we arrived, if you stayed out here."

"Oh," she said.

Marty added, "Ship's routine gets dull very fast. It's like going to sleep—only when you wake up, you'll be a bit tired. And you still dream while you're in hibernation. I know I'm going to dream of you!"

As she hugged him, Zeke sighed. "If you want to see what the process looks like, here's your chance," he said, pointing.

Jackson had already climbed into the first chamber and begun attaching the various devices that would monitor his body throughout the trip. Cal, one of the ship's two permanent on-board technicians, fitted the computer monitors to his head, made the final adjustments, then sealed the chamber. In seconds it filled with a swirling yellow gas that hid Jackson's features.

"He'll be asleep in a few moments," Zeke said. "The gas is a mild narcotic, and it's the first stage in the hibernation process."

"That's it?" Siona asked, amazed.

"That's it," Marty said. "Simple, huh? I bet I've done it a hundred times, now, and it's never hurt me once."

Siona giggled. "Well, you'd better tuck me in, Prince Charming."

"And I'll wake you with a kiss—just you wait!"

The technicians were just closing the top of Sylvie's chamber. "You're next," Zeke said to Siona.

"Which one is mine?" she asked.

"Here, next to me," Marty said. He helped her climb up into the hibernation chamber, then stood back as Cal and Harry fitted the little metal circlet around her head and attached small electrodes to her wrists. They eased the chamber's top down, and the yellow gas swirled over her face.

Marty was next, then Zeke, then the technicians themselves.

And as they all breathed the yellow gas, and their bodies began to slow down, each had different thoughts about the upcoming excavation.

Dr. Ezekiel Bones thought: *How can there be dragons? There must be a simple explanation I've missed. If only I could see it—*

Jackson Charles thought: *I hope his stomach holds out. I hate it when he doesn't take proper care of himself. If anything happens to him out here—*

Sylvie Pharr thought: *I must remember to get him to sign the release papers* before *anything interesting happens this time . . .*

Reelys thought: *I should be used to space travel by now, so why does it still bother me? I should have listened to my superiors and stayed on Earth—*

Marty Szigmond thought: *She's beautiful, and she loves me. Could this be the woman I'm going to marry?*

And Siona Jacobi thought: *Business before pleasure, old girl. Don't fall for him. You have a job to do, and jobs come first.* Jobs always came first.

Chapter Five

The receiver crackled with static, but Carter Simmons could still make out the words. He leaned forward, straining to hear.

"This is the starship *Ostrom*." the man's voice repeated. "Calling Beta Caloris IV. Come in, please."

"Sir?" said the technician monitoring the subspace radio. "Their ship is . . . *strange*. I've never seen an energy reading like it's putting out. And they're coming from the wrong direction—"

"What do you mean?" Simmons demanded.

"They're coming from deep space instead of the black hole station."

"Slowship or . . . invariance overdrive?" Simmons murmured to himself. He'd heard stories of IO ships and their ability to travel almost instantaneously between worlds, but he had never really believed them. Rumors of miracle technologies seldom turned out to be true. But if someone *did* have a working IO ship, it would be BEC. And if BEC thought the aboriginal tunnels important enough to send a ship equipped with their new IO drive, that meant he had really found something. He hoped he could get enough of a handle on it to do his career some good. After the disaster Camelot was turning into, he had a feeling his career might need a hand up.

"Let me talk to them," he said. It would be best to verify everything personally, he decided, to make sure they were who he thought they were. No use getting into a panic over a lost freighter, after all.

The technician set the controls, then said, "Go ahead, sir. Ready."

He cleared his throat and, in his most commanding voice, said: "To the starship *Ostrom*—this is Carter Simmons, planetary supervisor of Beta Caloris IV. Beta Caloris IV is a mining planet wholly owned and operated by the Panadium Trading and Mining Company, a subsidiary of the Bones Energy Corporation. Please state your business."

The receiver crackled. "This is Dr. Ezekiel Bones, Mr. Simmons. I am here on behalf of BEC to look into the aboriginal tunnels and artifacts you reported. Our ETA is two days. Please prepare suitable accommodation for a research crew of six."

"We have a guest house for visiting officials."

"That will do nicely, until we set up a camp of our own. *Ostrom* out."

The Knight Inquisitor meets his King, Simmons thought. Dr. Ezekiel Bones: He recognized that name from some of the newsvids he'd seen—Bones was the most famous archaeologist in all the universe.

And suddenly the BEC directive about alien artifacts made sense. Dr. Ezekiel Bones and the Bones Energy Corporation—somehow he'd never put the two together before.

I need a drink, Simmons thought. He ran a hand through his hair and felt the sweat beginning to trickle down his back and sides.

Dr. Bones nodded as he switched off the subspace radio. "I'm glad that's settled," he said. "We wouldn't want to arrive there and catch them by surprise."

"Do you want us to put you back in your hibernation chamber?" Harry offered. "Not much to do till we make orbit, sir. You might do well to sleep it away."

Zeke shook his head. "I want to be fully aware when we get there," he said. "My brain feels like oatmeal right now!"

"I'll get you something to drink," Cal said, rising. "I'm feeling that way myself."

Harry said, "You need to get your body back in balance. Sleeptanks play nasty games with your internal chemistry."

"I know," Zeke said, a trifle uncomfortably. His stomach was already starting to feel queasy.

Why does he always give me the dirty work? Felix Alonzo kept asking himself, as he trudged along the dark path to the guest house. He scuffed at the ground angrily. *I have better things to do than waste my time pissing Wagner to hell and back.*

Simmons had summoned him imperiously into his office twenty minutes before. There, as though he were laying down the Word of God, he had said: "Go tell Wagner that he has to get out of the guest house tomorrow. Executives from BEC are scheduled to arrive, and they'll want top quarters for themselves."

"Pardon, sir," he'd said in his most reasonable voice, "but Wagner won't be happy about that."

"It's your job to see that he *is* happy about it. These are his bosses as well as mine—tell him to keep that in mind. Otherwise, promise him whatever you have to to keep him cooperative."

Cooperative: That was an odd choice of words. Alonzo reflected on it as the guest house loomed nearer. Perhaps Simmons was starting to feel the pressure of a screwed-up job: Their production had fallen well below projected quotas for the last few months, and that wouldn't look good on his record.

Alonzo nodded happily. Not good at all.

Finally he reached the guest house, and the buzzer announced him to Wagner. When nothing happened, he leaned on the button.

It took the pilot a good ten minutes to get around to answering the door. When he did, he was dressed in gray company-issue coveralls, and looked like he'd been up for hours; he just hadn't bothered to answer the door.

"What do you want?" he growled.

"It's about time!"

"I'm on leave. Spit it out or bugger off."

"Carter Simmons sent me with a message for you. You have to move out of the guest house tomorrow morning."

Wagner frowned suddenly, and Alonzo noticed with a touch of panic that the pilot's fists were clenching and unclenching spasmodically.

"What do you mean, I have to leave?" Wagner said, in a very flat, very controlled voice.

"I'm sorry—it's Simmons's orders. There are BEC execs arriving tomorrow—"

Wagner jabbed a finger at Alonzo's chest. "Did it ever occur to you that I might *hate* being cooped up in a starship? That two weeks in guest houses every three months helps make up for what I have to suffer in space?"

"We'll move you to a place just as nice!"

"*Where?*" Wagner rumbled.

Alonzo smiled as the answer came to him. "The—ah—planetary supervisor's house." Hadn't Simmons said to promise Wagner anything to keep him happy? "He said so himself. He *wants* you to be happy."

Wagner began to smile. He clapped Alonzo on the back. "Okay," he said. "I'll try it, pal. I bet he lives even better than this!"

Felix just said, "Great." He knew Carter Simmons would be only too happy to move out to make room for Bill Wagner. The planetary supervisor could be such a generous man, when he had to be.

The last Knight of Komako knew trouble had come when his Mordred walked through the door whistling to himself. When Alonzo was happy it almost always meant more problems.

"What is it this time?" Simmons said. "Won't Wagner move?"

"Oh, yes, he agreed to move. He was a bit upset at first, but calmed down when I agreed to let him have what he thought were even better quarters."

"Better quarters?"

"Yours, sir."

Be calm. A Knight is always just. There is a suitable answer for every problem. "I suppose you had to," he said, after a moment of strangled silence. "He is, after all, quite important to us."

"Yes, sir."

"And sacrifices have to be made for the good of the company."

"That's right, sir."

Simmons himself was nodding now, and had even begun to smile. Suddenly Alonzo lost his happy look. "Since we've set up a precedent," the last Knight said, weighing the justice of it in his mind and finding it perfect, "I will simply move into your quarters for the duration. I trust you can find suitable accommodations for yourself either in the miners' barracks or in one of the other officers' houses."

"Yes, sir," Alonzo said, his face darkening with rage. He lost his perfect control for a second and his lip pulled back in an ugly sneer. He turned and strode from the room, slamming the door behind him.

Simmons began to laugh. *There is always justice*, he reminded himself. Giving up his house to Wagner for a week or so might even be worth it to finally annoy Alonzo, he thought. And it would certainly look good in the company record when he put it there. *Planetary supervisor sacrifices all for the good of his men*. He chuckled. Definitely good news.

When the *Heinrich Schliemann* landed two days later, Carter Simmons was there to greet it. He wore his Knighthood proudly, standing stiff backed, chin up, eyes gazing straight ahead. He wore his finest black uniform, neatly pressed, with the BEC insignia done in gold on the right breast pocket, and the Panadium Trading and Mining Corporation's silver star-and-rocket on the shoulder. Not even Alonzo looked so good, he thought.

He snuck a glance at his camp supervisor, who stood at his right side. Alonzo's uniform was utterly perfect too, but somehow its company gray seemed downstaged by the flash of Simmons's black; the eye came to the planetary supervisor *first*, and that was what he'd wanted.

As the shuttle's hatch swung open and its ramp extended, Simmons moved forward with a brisk stride and an easy expression. *I must make a good impression*, he thought.

And he knew he would. He'd always been good at these little corporate games of showmanship.

Chapter Six

Zeke was first through the hatch and onto the shuttle's ramp. The first thing that struck him was the smell: The air here held a touch of sulfur, and a touch of something else he couldn't quite identify. It left an unpleasant taste in the back of his mouth, but at least it was breathable, he thought. He'd worked on worlds where spacesuits were the uniform of the day, and he'd always hated the distance it placed between him and a site.

For a second he just stood there, looking at the gray-clouded sky, letting the warm breeze blow over him. *Half a day and I won't notice the smell*, he told himself. He'd spent enough time aboard Legion ships to be able to ignore any odor, given enough time.

There were people moving forward, demanding his attention. He turned to them and forced a happy greeting, trotting down the ramp. Jackson followed half a step behind.

A slightly overweight man with graying hair led the welcoming delegation. Zeke recognized him from the holocube: Carter Simmons, the planetary supervisor of mining operations. Simmons's uniform was neat, and he had a pleasant expression: Zeke had always valued first impressions, and Simmons gave him a moderately good one.

"Good day," the planetary supervisor said. "Welcome to Komako. You must be Dr. Bones?"

"Yes, and you must be Carter Simmons." Zeke. said, extending his hand.

Simmons shook it; his palm was damp but his grip was strong. "I'm delighted to meet you, Dr. Bones. I've, uh, heard a great deal about you."

"Really?"

He nodded. "We get all the newsvids out here—a bit slower than everyone else in the universe, but then galactic events aren't that pressing to us, are they?"

Zeke grinned easily: Simmons had a disarming quality about him. He decided he liked the man. "I would imagine not." He turned to his bodyguard. "This is my assistant, Jackson Charles."

"Mr. Charles," Simmons said, shaking hands again.

Zeke asked, "What was it you said? 'Welcome to Camelot?'"

Simmons laughed. "One of the privileges of being planetary supervisor is getting to name your planet, and I've christened Beta Caloris IV 'Komako.' It seems quite appropriate, in retrospect, considering the dragon statues we turned up."

"Indeed," Zeke said. He glanced over his shoulder to see the rest of his party emerging from the shuttle. They seemed eager, but a bit bleary eyed. He'd let them out of their hibernation chambers only a few hours before the trip down, and they hadn't fully recovered yet.

Sylvie Pharr emerged first—without her cameras; Zeke had packed them and put them in the shuttle cargo bay before he'd awakened her—followed by Siona and Marty, still glued hand-to-hand. Only Reelys seemed close to normal, drifting down the ramp with his'er gasbag half inflated in a sort of bounding step, part walk and part float.

"A pair of hlidskji? And a shri?" asked Simmons. "A very interesting group you have here."

"The shri is an expert on galactic history. Marty is an engineer, and Siona is his girlfriend. Sylvie is excavation holographer." As the others joined him, he introduced them to Simmons.

"Delighted to meet you," Simmons said, smiling at each with genuine warmth. "We're always glad to have company. Seeing the same faces day in and day out become a bit dreary after a while."

The man in the gray uniform beside Simmons cleared his throat.

"Oh yes," Simmons said. "I'm forgetting my camp supervisor, Felix Alonzo. Couldn't run the place without him."

"Pleased to meet you, sir," Alonzo said, and shook the hand Bones offered.

Zeke smiled back, trying to evaluate him and not really getting any strong impressions. "Glad to meet you, too."

"Felix," Simmons said, "why don't you make sure their baggage gets taken to the guest house at once, while I show them the way up?"

"Yes, sir," Alonzo said, but Zeke couldn't help but notice the half-second glare he gave his boss.

He doesn't like being an errand boy, Zeke thought, then did a double take. *Simmons had deliberately snubbed him— perhaps a bit of stress between the two?* He'd have to keep an eye on Alonzo, he thought; Simmons didn't strike him as the sort who would hold grudges without cause.

"Well, enough idle chatter," Simmons said. "You all must be exhausted from your journey, and I imagine you'll want to freshen up before dinner. You will do me the honor of being my guests this evening, I hope? The robochef has been cooking up a storm all day, and promises something special in honor of this occasion."

"Sounds terrific," Sylvie said. "And perhaps you'd let me interview you a bit later?"

"An interview? Why, I don't see why not." He paused, studying her. "Haven't I seen you somewhere before? On the vids, perhaps?"

She nodded. "I do a lot of reporting for VCI."

"I thought so. We can discuss it tonight, over dinner." He turned and indicated a jumpcar parked ten feet away. "This way, please. I'll fly you up myself."

The jumpcar whined from the extra weight as they took off, but Simmons kept insisting it was up to the burden. "All the equipment here has been enhanced," he said. "In case of emergencies, the jumpcars serve as evacuation vehicles—they can carry over five thousand kilos each, according to the specs. We've never had them up that high, of course, since we've never had any real emergencies here—but it's always best to be prepared."

"Indeed." Zeke peered out the window, at rolling grasslands which stretched as far as the eye could see. "Why was the guest house set out here, instead of closer to the camp itself?"

"It's mostly used by shuttle pilots, and they tend to want to stay near their ships. And, of course, they're a bit—well—*odd*, if you know what I mean. Being in space so long does things to people's minds. It's always been company policy to keep the pilots and the miners separated as much as possible."

Zeke nodded. "I have a few other questions, if you don't mind. I'm afraid BEC's files on Beta Caloris—*Komako*, rather—are a bit sketchy. The initial surveys didn't even mention how much of the continent had been explored."

"It's all been photographed, and core samples were taken from several hundred sites. This one proved to have the highest concentrations of ore and precious minerals, so that's where we set up. Everything is in my computer, if you want to have a look at it."

"And then there's the native life-forms. There's nothing but grass out there?" He turned again to the endless stretch of green, which covered hill and flatland alike.

"Not a thing on land, not an insect, not a grub nor an earthworm. If you get a chance, take a walk beyond the camp's boundaries—it's quite a strange sensation, being out there all alone. Rather eerie, I guess you'd say, though I find it rather pleasant, myself. I take walks when the pressures of administration get to me."

"It's early still," Zeke said. It was hard to tell with the cloud cover, but he guessed several hours of daylight still remained. "Do you have time to circle around and show us your camp before dinner?"

"If everyone's up to it," Simmons said. "Dinner won't be for at least three hours, and I can always have the robochef keep things hot, if necessary. Do you want the air tour?"

There was a chorus of assents from the back.

"All right then," Simmons said. He swung the jumpcar around and headed it back the way they'd come. They passed over the runway and the two shuttles parked there, and then over a series of low, rolling hills completely covered by more of the grass.

As they topped a last rise, Zeke saw a wide valley below. Two open pits and the beginnings of a third were the most noticeable features. To the far left clustered a group of squarish buildings and a high tower with a receiver dish on top. To the far right stood several hangarlike buildings. Beyond them stretched neatly plowed fields, the brown earth between orderly rows of plants a striking contrast to the green of the surrounding countryside.

Simmons circled around, naming the various buildings as offices and houses for camp officials as they passed over them. "That one's mine," he said as he pointed to one of the smaller buildings. "We'll be eating there. Bill Wagner, the *Constellation*'s pilot and captain, will be joining us as well."

"The *Constellation*, that's the freighter in orbit?" Sylvie asked.

"Yes," Simmons said. "Wagner was scheduled to leave in three days, but it looks as though he'll be with us a bit longer than that. The *Constellation* is having a few problems with her engines, and my technicians are up there working on her now. Nothing major, they say, just time-consuming. Various things need to be relined and recalibrated—much too technical for me to follow."

Sylvie made sympathetic noises.

Now they were passing over the two largest mining pits, which seemed empty. From there they headed for the third, which was much shallower—just beginning. Here hundreds of humans and robots worked. Equipment rumbled everywhere, raising clouds of gray dust as thick as any fog Zeke had ever seen on Earth.

And yet there was something odd about the scene.

Reelys was the one who spotted it. "There are no !xaka!," s/he said.

"That's right," Simmons said. He looked at Zeke. "Wasn't that in your reports?"

"No."

"Odd," he said. "I don't know why, but it's always been company policy just to use humans and robots—less tension that way, I suppose. Though I've worked with them in the past, the !xaka! never really struck me as good team players—and that's what the people are here, a team. A sort of family, if you will."

Zeke nodded, but said nothing. It made sense. He was glad for a second that he hadn't been able to reach his !xaka! friend, Kadak!xa.

Next Simmons swung around and took them over the miners' camp. "The white buildings are barracks," he said. "Normally there are two people to a room, but we have a few empties now; I haven't been requesting replacement miners for those who've left or died. Married miners are in the houses to the left."

"Died?" Zeke said.

"There have been a few accidents over the last six months—just after I shut down the first pit because of the tunnels. It was to be expected, I suppose. I had everyone on half-shift, and that left too many with too much free time. So they did some stupid things, and a few of them got killed. Sometimes they're so much like naughty children . . ." He sighed.

Zeke turned his attention to the miners' camp. It was without a doubt the most civilized one he had ever seen—and he'd seen quite a few during his days with the Legion of Ares. He'd had to help crush several miners' rebellions and union strikes, and though he'd fought against them every time, he'd always sympathized with the miners. But the Legion didn't get paid for its morality; it got paid to do the dirty work for anyone with money. It had been an unhappy time of his life in many ways,

Zeke thought, though some good had come of it. He'd met all of his closest friends in the Legion—Reelys, Sylvie, Marty. Even Jackson, though his bodyguard had only been a child at the time.

In those days, the average mining planet had wallowed in squalor. Here, things looked vastly different: The streets had been paved, small flower gardens splashed bits of red and gold with colorful exotic blooms, and clothes hung out to dry on lines. It might have been any settlement on a frontier world. Children ran playing in the side yards and fields, and Zeke even saw a couple of dogs.

"It looks quite nice here," he said. "I don't think I've ever seen a mining operation quite like this one."

"There's none like it in the galaxy," Simmons said proudly. "I've been trying out some of the more progressive theories of mining supervision, and I've been getting good results." He paused. "Have you ever been to Old Tartus, by any chance?"

"Yes," Zeke said simply. The name brought back a slew of unpleasant memories, which he quickly shunted aside. The Legion job on Old Tartus had been a quick and messy operation, a matter of blasting through barricades, killing quite a few union leaders, and forcing the miners back to work in unsafe underground mines. Cave-ins had been a daily happening there, and literally hundreds of men and women had died every year as a result. Luckily things had improved since then—in realtime, it had been more than three decades ago; to Zeke, however, it had only been a handful of years, and his memories were still vivid.

"Then you know some of what it was like," Simmons said. "I was born on Old Tartus during the worst of its days."

Zeke nodded; he'd read that in Simmons's file. It explained a lot—how he had worked his way out of the mines, won a scholarship to study off world, and finally returned as a low-level supervisor for the Panadium Trading and Mining Company. He had a high efficiency rating, and good marks all around. He'd been a career man, and Beta Caloris IV had been his first assignment as planetary supervisor. If he made good here, there was no telling how far he might rise.

Zeke said, "So you've been working to make things better for miners all your life. Very commendable. I only wish there had been more like you, and sooner."

Silence followed after that; perhaps he'd touched on a sore point, Zeke thought. He didn't know what to say.

Finally Sylvie asked, "How many people are there on Beta Caloris IV? Komako, rather?"

"Twelve hundred and forty-six, counting the children." Simmons made a second pass over the barracks, pointing out the school and the church this time. "I'm afraid that's about all there is to see," he said. "We're a bit short of tourist attractions. Was there anything I left out?"

"To tell you the truth," Zeke said, "I've been cooped up in the shuttle for the past four days, and I could really use a chance to get out and walk enough to stretch my legs."

"Me too," Sylvie said, and the others echoed her sentiments.

Simmons said, "In that case, would you all like to see the first tunnel, the one I took holos of? You could take a walk through the west pit."

"That would be a great start!" Zeke said.

Simmons changed course and angled back toward the first pit. When it suddenly yawned beneath them, he circled the jumpcar down and landed it in the pit's middle, next to a row of huge, dormant machines. Zeke recognized them as rock-crunchers from the huge intake chamber on one end. They looked like they'd been sitting idle for some time, from the thick layer of gray dust that had settled on them.

"I stopped all our operations here, per instructions," Simmons said, as he powered down the jumpcar's engine. "I started the new south pit to keep the men busy. Since the tunnels are all at low levels, I didn't think that would do any harm." It was a statement, but it seemed to hang on a questioning note.

"I shouldn't think it would be a problem," Zeke said. He sensed more than saw the planetary supervisor's relief. *Probably worried that he should have shut everything down and kept it shut down*, he thought. He added, "Like you said, it was best to keep everyone working."

"Exactly," Simmons said. "Idle miners are nothing but trouble."

He opened the jumpcar's doors, and everyone climbed out, stretching and looking at the towering stone walls around them. Jackson let out a low whistle.

"Quite a place," Sylvie murmured.

Simmons went directly to the jumpcar's cargo compartment. "Open," he said, and the little door slid aside. He started pulling out bright yellow helmets and distributing them.

"For safety reasons, I really must ask you all to wear hard hats," he said. He set one on his own head as though underscoring his order. "The tunnels are in the pit's northern wall, and sometimes rockfalls occur there. Servos in the hard hats will warn of that, so you should have plenty of time to get out of the way, if necessary."

Zeke took his hard hat and slipped it on. The sizing band inside adjusted itself to fit his head with a click.

"Where are the tunnels?" he said.

"There." Simmons pointed to the left, and Zeke turned to see a pair of holes leading into the pit's wall. They were small, almost lost in the hugeness of the wall.

Zeke started for them at once, Simmons at his side, the others following. The tunnels were about five meters up, Zeke estimated as he drew close. The straightness of their sides and the way the tunnel roofs curved up in an even semi-circle left little doubt as to their origin: certainly carved out of the rock by sentient creatures.

"Interesting," he said. "How can I get up there?"

"There was a ladder around here somewhere," Simmons said, glancing around. Finally he spotted it and pointed. "There it is, next to the wall."

"Better let me go up first," Marty said. "No telling how safe it is. I'll take a quick look-see and let you know if we'll need to reinforce the walls and ceilings before entering."

"No need," Simmons said. "I had it checked months ago—didn't want it to cave in before I got my instructions. The camp geologist pronounced it perfectly safe. It seems the saurians—if, indeed, that's what the aboriginals were—built these tunnels to last for millennia."

"Good thinking," Zeke said. "I'll go up with Jackson. The rest of you should wait here—walk around, get your land legs again."

"Thanks heaps!" Sylvie said. "I didn't come here to watch you have all the fun!"

"It's not that," Zeke said. "I just don't want an army walking through the site before we have a chance to holograph everything *in situ*. Things are more likely to be moved or broken by accident in a crowd."

Sylvie sighed. "I guess you're right," she said. "That wasn't me talking, Doc—I'm just tired."

"Everyone is," Zeke said. He turned to Jackson. "Let's get that ladder!"

"Sure thing."

As they strolled over to get it, Jackson whispered, "We're being watched. Two people standing on the top wall opposite us."

"They're probably just curious. As Simmons said, new faces are rare here, and they probably want a look at us."

"You're much too trusting," Jackson replied. He lifted one end of the ladder; Zeke took the other. They started back and Zeke took the opportunity to glance at the two people Jackson had spotted. They stood on the opposite side of the quarry, on the rim of the south wall, where they could see the whole excavation team.

"They could be anybody," Jackson said. "For all we know, there could be a lot of unhappy miners here. You *did* shut down most of their mining operations, after all. And a couple of well-placed explosives would bring down this whole wall, burying us—and Simmons, too, if they had a grudge against him."

"You worry too much."

"Tell me that next time I save your skin."

They levered the ladder into place and for the moment their discussion was forgotten. Zeke scrambled up first, carrying one of the pocket lights Simmons gave them, with Jackson almost on his heels.

As he stepped into the first tunnel and shone the light across the walls, Zeke finally knew it wasn't a hoax: The place was *old*. It looked old, and it *felt* old. Carbon dating would give them the exact age later.

A thick layer of dust coated everything. He could still make out several trails of human footprints on the floor, weaving among the various dust-coated artifacts that lay there. And, as he moved forward slowly, cautiously, feeling his way so he wouldn't tread on anything important, the dust puffed up in little clouds around him.

"Whose footprints are those?" Jackson asked, pointing.

"Probably the geologist's," Zeke said. He prowled ahead, shining his light across the walls. "And Simmons's, and the miners who came in here before they realized it was more than a natural cave."

"Seems like an awful lot of them came in here. And did you notice the draft?" Jackson paused, turning slightly, eyes closed. "I can feel a breeze on my face. The tunnel must go back quite a way if it has another surface opening."

Zeke grinned. "An opening like the one next door?"

"Oh." He paused. "Still, you never know till it's all explored and mapped out. We'll have to set up lights so we can see everything."

"And we'll have to sift the dust and dirt," Zeke said. "No telling what's been buried in here."

Something dark and shiny caught his eyes. He knelt. It looked like a small pool of water, and when he touched it with his finger, he felt dampness. Taking a small servo from his belt, he moved it slowly over the spot.

"Grade 3 petrochemical," it chirped a moment later.

"That's machine oil," Jackson said.

"Odd thing to find in here."

"Perhaps our geologist brought equipment with him."

"Or perhaps someone else had a robot up here. That stain's fresh; the dust would have covered it by now if it had been here very long."

"Take a look at these!" Jackson called from the back corner.

Zeke crossed over to join him. On a shelf cut into the wall lay a series of small featherlike objects. Zeke touched one; it felt cool and smooth, glasslike. One side had a sharp edge—a cutting tool of some sort? Next to it lay a pile of jumbled glass shards; whatever it had been, it had shattered. Perhaps it could be pieced together later by an expert in pottery restoration.

Oddly, though, Zeke noticed that the dust on the shelf seemed to have been recently disturbed, as though someone had run his hand across it. Considering the amount of dust in the pit, the shelf certainly should have been covered much more deeply. They weren't far enough inside the tunnel for it to have escaped the dust.

"What do you think broke it?" Jackson said. "The blasting?"

"Probably. I'm going to have to talk to Simmons about that, get him to cut it out entirely."

Jackson grinned. "Did you get a look at the pit's walls? There's no other way to get the ore out. He's not going to be happy."

"I know. I'll deal with it later." Zeke shone his light toward the back of the room. A huge arched passageway led into another chamber. "As you said, no telling how far back the tunnels go. We're really going to have our work cut out for us here."

"Speaking of later, there will be time enough for exploring tomorrow," Jackson said. "If we keep the others waiting outside much longer, they'll lynch us when we get back!"

"Let's go, then," he said. "I've seen enough for now. I'm convinced it's a real site."

"But not real dragons, huh?" Jackson grinned.

"We'll see. Let's just say I'm keeping an open mind. It's a big universe, and anything is possible—no matter how unlikely."

As the various humans and aliens climbed back into the jumpcar below, Felix Alonzo moved back from the north pit's rim. He headed toward the company cantina, and Killian fell in step beside him.

"Well?" Killian said. "What did you think?"

Alonzo shrugged. "We're going to have to bug the tunnels. I can't plan unless I know what *they're* planning first."

"I can do that tonight," Killian said.

"No. Wait a few days, until they've stirred up the dust inside. We don't want them seeing your footprints, do we?"

"No, sir!"

"And," Alonzo said, warming to his plot, "you're to keep everything else at low profile. I want Bones to get too preoccupied with his work to notice what's going on around him. And by then it'll be too late."

The last Knight of Camelot knew something was wrong. His King had been silent throughout most of the evening meal, and afterward had asked to see his Knight alone in his office.

Only when the door had closed did he speak, and then it was with a troubled voice. "I'm afraid I'm going to have to ask you to shut down the new south pit, too," he said.

"What!" the last Knight cried, for a moment forgetting his composure. "Why?"

"A number of the artifacts in the tunnel have been shattered by blasting."

"So you want me to shut down *everything?*"

Bones nodded. "I'm afraid so—at least for the time being. You can start a new one twenty kilometers away—not a meter closer. Shuttle the men there and back as necessary."

"I know you think these artifacts are important," Simmons said, "but you must be realistic. If a mining

planet isn't paying its way, it's going to be shut down—
that's only common sense. And unless we can continue
with our operations, we're not going to make a profit this
year. This quarter's already shot—we haven't dug enough
ore to pay our people's salaries, let alone the operating
costs. And with these new restrictions—!"

"I'll see to it that everyone here is *guaranteed* their pay
and their job," Bones said. "Once we've established the
size of the site, you will be allowed to continue mining in
the clear areas. I think that's fair."

"Unfortunately, I'm not in a position to do anything
about it. But I intend to log my protests with the mining
company."

The King nodded gravely. "I know you're also concerned about your career," he said. "I'm aware of the fact
that this may look bad on your record."

"May? Trust me. It *will.*"

"But you must also realize there are things more important than any one man, or even any one company. Information is one. We learn from the past; we have to in
order to keep growing and surviving as a species."

The last Knight frowned, and fought down his anger.
A Knight is the master of his emotions, he reminded himself.

At last he leaned back and said, "I have a story for you.
Once there was a little boy who lived on a horribly brutal
mining planet. Now, this little boy was different from
other planet brats. He thought a lot, and he liked to read,
and he wanted to know everything about everything in
the universe. So he fought and he bribed and he literally
clawed his way out of the miners' ghetto. Both of his parents *died* serving that mining company, and that didn't
stop him. He wanted up, and he wanted out, and he was
determined to have it. Finally he got his chance, and

made it off-planet to some very private schools on company money. Do you follow me so far?"

"Yes." The King leaned back, listening.

"Schools are very political places. They polarize young minds against authority. While he was there, the little boy—now a young man—came to realize that the only way to subvert authority was to join it, rise to the top, and make it *his* authority, doing *his* will. That young man was me, Dr. Bones.

"And I've always been driven by the need to reshape this company to my views. I've always been driven by the fear of ending up as my parents did. *Don't interfere with my chance to change things.*

"Information is fine for those who are time-rich, like you. You don't have to sweat in the mines on Old Tartus, worrying if this will be your last day of life. You don't have to work double- or triple-shift hours just to pay for the hovel the company rents to you. *Those* are the realities of a miner's life. I have to deal with things I can see and hold and use. My success here is what will reshape the lives of my company's people, not some ancient garbage that aliens forgot to sweep out of their tunnels before they died!"

"Would it help," Bones asked softly, "if I guaranteed you a job with BEC if you get fired as a result of my orders here?"

"No," he said. "Weren't you listening? If I wanted another job, I could get one with any mining company around. I want *this* job. I've spent my life at it, and I don't mean to stop now."

"I'm not without influence," Bones said. "You won't be fired here. I can guarantee you that much."

"But what about my career?" he said. "Not even you can guarantee promotions. They go to those whose records show they merit them. Besides, I'm a company man, Dr. Bones, and in company politics promises like yours are easily forgotten."

"I'm sorry," Zeke Bones said. "We must all do what we're called to do. If it truly means that much to you— you'll find a way."

"I'll think about it," Simmons said.

"I'm afraid that's the best I can do." He offered the last Knight his hand. Simmons shook it, but a bit sadly.

And as he watched Bones go, he wondered if Bones were telling the truth. Would Bones really have given him a job if the company fired him? He'd lived too long among the back-stabbing and the double-dealing of corporate politics to believe Bones completely. And yet something made him want to trust the young archaeologist. . . .

Simmons shook his head. One thing the company prided itself in was loyalty. If Alonzo ever found out about his conversation with Bones, even though he'd turned down his offer, Simmons knew he'd have to watch his back.

Using a superior's indiscretion was, after all, how Simmons himself had made planetary supervisor. He didn't want Alonzo getting to the top the same way.

Chapter Seven

Zeke Bones rose early the next day. The guest house lay quiet around him, and he assumed he was the first to waken. When he glanced at the clock, though, he was surprised to find it well into the morning, far later than he would have guessed. *The hibernation chamber*, he thought, *still catching up with me*.

Quickly he showered and changed, and headed for the dining room. Hopefully the others would be up and waiting for him.

A robot butler dressed in a black tuxedo greeted him as he stepped into the hall.

"Good morning, sir," it said. "I trust you slept well. There is a gentleman waiting here to see you."

"Oh?" Zeke said. "Who is it?"

"A Mr. Simmons, sir. The planetary supervisor."

Good thing I left orders not to be disturbed, Zeke thought with a chuckle. He said, "Where is he?"

"The dining room, sir. If you would follow me."

Zeke trailed after the robot through the living room and into the huge, ornate dining room. Here, an outsized synthawood table sat, surrounded by high-backed chairs. The crystal chandelier and plush gray carpeting underfoot completed the setting: opulent, almost too much so for Zeke's tastes.

Simmons had seated himself at the far end of the table and was just finishing the plate of waffles in front of him. He waved Zeke to the chair at his left with his fork.

"I came to tell you," he said between bites, "that all mining operations have ended for now at the south pit. I became a bit hungry and ordered myself breakfast. I hope you don't mind."

"Not at all," Zeke said, feeling a moment's elation: Simmons had actually seen the sense of his argument after all, and acted on it immediately. "I assume you're moving to a new location?"

"That's right." Simmons took a last bite and dialed himself more waffles from the robochef. "Anything for you?"

"What you're having looks good to me."

He dialed a second serving, then continued. "There's another ore deposit about twenty-eight kilometers due east of here. It's in the same valley, and the survey geologists said it was part of the same rock formation. The ore just proved a tad richer here, so we set up here first. Once these pits were played out, we would've moved there next anyway."

"Good. And your men?"

"Once the equipment's in place, we'll be flying everyone over on cargo platforms. At least for the time being. We may just move the whole camp—though that's a big decision."

"Frankly, I thought there might be more problems than that."

"There's been grumbling, of course. But there's grumbling every time anything changes. No, I think my men had pretty well resigned themselves to coming changes once the tunnels were found. No one expected you to arrive this quickly, though."

"I'm almost always on a tight schedule. Luckily I had a few free months to sneak off for a working vacation."

The robochef chose that moment to deliver food. Simmons sighed contendedly at the waffles. Zeke picked at his food, not feeling all that hungry, but knowing he had to eat: Reelys and Jackson would insist.

As he poured butter and syrup on his, Simmons looked up and said, almost as an afterthought, "Or did you mean logistical problems? *Those* I have plenty of."

Zeke looked up. "Oh?"

"The crunchers and bulldozers left at dawn. They should arrive at the new site sometime this afternoon, and ground clearing is scheduled to start tomorrow morning. That still left several hundred miners with nothing to do today, since they couldn't start work without equipment supporting them. So I gave everyone except the drivers the day off. It's nothing you should be concerned with . . . unless they bother you."

"Oh, I doubt if they will."

Simmons shrugged. "They're a curious lot. I imagine you'll be playing to an audience all day—that is, I assumed you were all going out to have a look at the tunnels today."

"That was the general idea." Zeke paused, listening. Yes—he definitely heard stirrings from the other rooms. His friends were finally starting to awaken. Knowing how much the hibernation chambers had taken out of them made him sympathetic—five days later, he still felt the aftereffects. Sleep remained the best cure.

A moment later, Sylvie wandered in, followed a few seconds later by Jackson. Sylvie was stylishly decked out in a cream-colored jumpsuit that somehow managed to accentuate her curves, rather than hide them. Jackson wore a sturdy brown shirt and pants, practical garb for down-and-dirty work in trenches.

And both of them looked bleary eyed, though Sylvia hid it better. Zeke pretended not to notice: best to keep them from thinking about the way they felt.

"What do you want for breakfast?" he asked.

"Coffee," Sylvia said. She flopped into the first empty chair at the table, and Jackson took the next. "I'd *kill* for a cup."

Even from a distance she smelled terrific; Zeke couldn't help but notice. The faintest touch of some spicy perfume lingered around her. It sent prickles down his spine.

"Soyfee will have to do," he said, after a delicious second. He punched it up on the robochef's instruction menu. "What about you, Jackson?"

"The same," Jackson said. He cradled his head in his hands and groaned. "I think the trip here just caught up to me."

"Do either of you want something solid to eat?"

"Anything with sugar," Sylvie said. "And megadoses of caffeine."

"You might," Simmons suggested between bites of his waffle, "try some of our homegrown Lazerby melons. They really are quite sweet this time of year."

Reelys floated in a second later. His'er mantle almost glowed, the swirled patterns on it sharp and bright. "Good day, Ezekiel," s/he said. "I heard you talking and thought you might want more company. And good day, Sylvie and Jackson. And you too, Mr. Simmons."

By the time everyone had greeted him'er, Marty and Siona appeared as well, hand in hand, looking bright eyed and happy. *At least as bright-eyed as they can look*, Zeke thought, considering their black eyes with white pupils.

"When's everyone else gonna be ready to go?" Marty said. "We've been waiting for hours!"

"We took a walk," Siona said. "It's a beautiful day."

"After breakfast," Zeke said, grinning at everyone around the table. "Right, guys?"

Jackson groaned again. Zeke thought he heard him murmur, "*Damn mutant metabolisms.*"

Half an hour later, once the robot butler had cleared the table of what little remained from breakfast, everyone rose at once by some unspoken agreement and moved for the door.

A featureless slab of gray-white cumulus clouds covered the sky, but the warm breeze, open air, and seemingly endless sprawl of green-covered hills was more than enough to cheer anyone's spirits.

Indeed, as Siona had said, it was a beautiful Komakoan day.

Things are definitely looking better, Jackson thought, taking a deep breath. He ignored the bitter taste the air left in the back of his mouth.

He turned his attention back to Zeke.

Simmons was telling his boss, "I'm afraid I'm going to have to leave. I have a lot of equipment to look after, and the robodrones are supposed to start shunting cargo up to the *Constellation* today. So if you have any questions, please feel free to call my assistant, Felix Alonzo. He'll be able to take care of everything you might need."

"I'll do that," Zeke said.

Simmons turned and headed for a small white jumpcar. It sat next to the larger black 'car he'd turned over—reluctantly, Jackson had thought—to Zeke for the duration of their stay.

What was it he'd said? Robodrones would be shuttling ore to the freight in orbit? Jackson looked south, toward the shuttleport. Two silver daggerlike ships were just disappearing into the clouds—the first of the little robot shuttles, he guessed. *Just as well,* he thought. *It'll keep Simmons off our backs.* At least, it would until the *Constellation* was ready to leave.

By then, with a little luck, they'd have their excavation up and running. Once the dig actually began, nothing would be able to deter Zeke from his task. Jackson smiled. His boss had the tenacity of a brainlocked !xaka! at times.

Zeke called for everyone's attention, and the whole party gathered around him, listening expectantly.

"There's going to be a lot to do," Zeke said. "Siona, are you willing to lend a hand, too, until we get everything going?"

"Of course!" she said. "You'd have a hard time keeping me away, Zeke! I didn't come halfway across the universe to sit and watch. Just ask Marty!" She gave him a quick squeeze.

"What she said," Marty told Zeke, grinning.

Zeke couldn't help but grin back. "I'll want you two to start unloading the *Heinrich Schliemann.* With all the robots around, you shouldn't have much trouble. You know what we'll need to set up camp."

"Right, Doc. Leave it to us."

Zeke then looked to Jackson and Reelys. "We'll need a good place to set up our camp, too. Someplace close to all the tunnels."

"I know, I know," Jackson said. "You always want the same thing: high ground in case of floods, a nice breeze in case of hot weather, level ground so Marty can put together all the prefab buildings he's got sectioned in the shuttle's cargo hold. We've done this a hundred times before, Zeke!"

"But," Bones said, "it pays to make sure."

Reelys added, "Trust us, Ezekiel, we know what we are doing."

"That leaves Sylvie and me." He glanced over at her. "Are you up to taking some pictures today?"

"It's my job, Doc. I'm always ready for it. *If* you'll let me unpack my cameras from the shuttle this time?"

He laughed. "You could always do what the ancient archaeologists did and make pen-and-ink sketches of all the artifacts."

"Today I'm a holographer, not an artist."

He gave her a puzzled look. "Oh?"

She laughed. "Give me a week to get my land legs and ask me again."

Marty said, "No sense wasting time standing around here." He turned to Jackson. "Do you still have the ignition block for our jumpcar?"

Jackson felt its hardness through the shirt pocket he'd dropped it into.

"Yep," he said.

"Then let's go, already!"

With Jackson at the wheel and the others chatting around him, Zeke found himself staring moodily out the window. The alien grass made the scenery endlessly monotonous: Somehow, he found hill after hill of rounded greenery a depressing sight. Even on Earth, where kudzu had taken over, shapes broke the smoothness of the vegetation. Here the alien grass had just grown wild. If there had ever been anything else, all traces had utterly vanished over the millennia.

"A very successful lifeform," Reelys said.

Zeke glanced at the shri. "What makes you say that?"

"It has found its niche and filled it."

"I don't know . . . somehow, I think its success is really a dead-end."

"How is that?"

"There is no challenge for it here: It exists merely to continue existing. There is no struggle for survival with other plants, so it has no reason to continue to develop and change. Without subvarieties, it's going to be fragile in the long run—what happens when there's a climactic change and it proves unable to cope?"

"It would be killed."

"Exactly."

The landing strip had appeared before them, with the two shuttles parked near the storage sheds at the far end. Robots moved there, piling huge square ingots of smelted iron in stacks for easy storage in the robodrones when they returned.

Jackson put the jumpcar down with professional ease, twenty meters from the *Heinrich Schliemann*. The doors popped open and everyone piled out, Zeke following Reelys.

Once on land, he touched a servo at his collar. It beamed a recognition signal at the shuttle, which responded with a low beep, then a pause for the password.

Zeke said, "Open sesame." The shuttle's cargo hatch silently unlocked and began to swing open.

Sylvie said. "You'd better have put my cameras in a safe place!"

• • •

An hour and a half later, with Marty and Siona left to unload the shuttle and Sylvie's holocameras found and fully checked out as working, Zeke had Jackson head for the north pit.

After he and Sylvie had unloaded their various bags of equipment, Jackson took off, heading for a quick pass-over of the terrain surrounding the mining pits. Zeke had little doubt that he and Reelys would find the perfect place for their camp.

He put on the hard hat Simmons had given him and gave the pit a quick once-over. In stronger daylight, it still seemed much the same: bleak, somehow desolate without its work crews. The slowly rusting machinery only added to that impression.

Sylvie activated her cameras one by one. They rose and hovered around her, lenses focusing and unfocusing as their little computers ran start-up diagnostics. Finally everything seemed to check out; Sylvie folded up her bag and tucked it under her arm.

"Ready?" Zeke asked, shouldering his own bag of equipment—lights mostly, but also a few brushes for removing dirt and dust. "Don't forget your hard hat."

"Not till after I do my stand-up," Sylvie said. "I'll be perfectly safe here. Why don't you go ahead up the ladder? I'll be done by the time you get there, and I want to holo you climbing into the tunnel mouth. 'Intrepid adventurer challenging the unknown' and all that."

Zeke turned and headed for the tunnels without anoth-er word; behind him, he heard Sylvie starting her usual hype about the mysteries of the dragon statues, the histo-ry of Bones and his team, and what they hoped to accom-plish by coming here. Zeke knew it didn't really matter at this point whether or not he objected to Sylvie making a documentary on the side. If he had, Sylvie would just have pointed out that she had a living to make, and shooting him climbing into the tunnel was a small enough favor in return for her work in taking pictures of all his artifacts. Which was perfectly true, he realized. But with the tunnels so close, and his urge to explore them so great, the longing to rush, to see what mysteries they held burned in him like an unquenchable fire.

He clipped a pair of bright, glowing flashtubes to his belt, then started up the ladder.

Chapter Eight

"Look at them," Felix Alonzo said with disgust, "scurrying around like ants. They actually think the stuff in the caves *is* important."

Bill Wagner shrugged his broad shoulders. "Perhaps to them it is. It's certainly valuable to us."

It was late evening, but a hundred meters below, the slowly lengthening shadows on the floor of the north pit seethed with movement as robots and people shunted equipment toward the mouths of the two tunnels. A wide metal ramp led up into the tunnel where the first two dragon statues had been found. If Bones and his team had noticed Alonzo and Wagner watching from the pit's wall, they paid no attention.

Alonzo sat and continued to stare. Something exciting had clearly happened below, and he wanted to know what it was.

In the two weeks since Bones and his people had been here, they'd done little of interest—just worked at building their excavation. Now it had a certain logic to it: They had placed five large, prefabricated buildings in a little cluster halfway between the north and west mining pits, on a little hill. They used the five mostly as storage sheds, with shelves full of artifacts removed from the various tunnels. And there were a number of work stations for Bones and his people.

Alonzo knew their camp in intimate detail: Simmons had volunteered him to help set everything up. It had been three days of backbreaking labor, many extra hours of supervising robots and miners, and more inconvenience than he cared to think about to get those buildings set up, ramps into the tunnels built, and all their lights and generators and other, more specialized equipment installed.

"Look," Wagner said, pointing unnecessarily. "More of the dragon statues. They must have opened up a room you missed."

Alonzo cursed. Sure enough, Bones's men were carrying several more of the statues down the ramp. "Those should've been ours!" he said. He counted—was it four? And they were carrying other artifacts out as well.

"It's not too late," Wagner said. "I haven't gone yet."

Alonzo looked curiously at the pilot. "You mean—steal those?"

"Sure," Wagner said. "Why not? If you're not daring, you'll never get anywhere. You know I'm not scheduled to leave until the day after tomorrow—if you were to send those statues up by robodrone before then, they could be stowed aboard the *Constellation* in plenty of time. I have a Security Two rating. They'd never think to search me." He laughed.

Alonzo chewed his lip and thought about it. The plan did make a certain amount of sense . . . and Bones and his people were noticeably lax about their security. . . .

It would take some thought, but it could be done. And when he thought of the bonus for more of the dragon statues, it made his mouth water.

"I'll do it!" he said at last.

Wagner clapped him on the back and laughed. "I knew you would. You're a greedy son of a bitch, and I like you for it!"

Inside the first cave, Zeke was taking his first break of the day. It had been the most hectic of the two weeks they'd been on Camelot. That morning, they'd done a few tests on the tunnels, determining that most of the walls had hollow spaces behind them. They'd removed a small section of the back wall just before lunch—a lunch that Zeke had completely forgotten to eat—and revealed another section of tunnels.

And this one looked as though it had been recently occupied: Artifacts lay everywhere, dozens of them, some as though they had been set down only moments before, with their owners intending to pick them up after a quick break. Only the thin layer of dust over everything indicated the passed centuries since anything in the room had been touched.

Zeke had drawn a quick, surprised breath—and ordered everyone back except Sylvie. And, with him holding a light, they'd gone together into the room.

Everything looked to be in perfect condition. Sylvie's holocameras buzzed through the room, here pausing over a dragon statue, there hovering around plastic cubes, flitting back and forth until precise records of everything had been made. In places the artifacts were so close together he was afraid of trying to step lest he slip and accidentally break one.

"Incredible," he kept murmuring.

From outside, he heard Jackson and Reelys discussing the find in excited voices. He shut them out and focussed his attention on the task at hand.

Only when Sylvia was done, three hours later, did Zeke dare to touch anything. He'd run his hand down the spine of one of the dragon statues, knowing that they were real for the first time.

Simmons and his men hadn't been in here; the dust lay undisturbed. This room sat exactly as the aboriginals had left it.

He felt the excitement, the rush of adrenaline, the pure *joy* of the moment. Times like this were what made him love archaeology.

Next, after everything had been holographed, came the study period. Zeke had come to the conclusion that the aboriginals' culture could never truly be appreciated here, and the artifacts and his notes and holos would all have to be sent to Griynsh for the Galactic Museum's scholars and researchers to study. Perhaps, in time, they would dispatch their own survey and research team to continue the work he would barely be able to begin in the few months he would spend here.

Outside, he called Simmons. The pocket communicator flickered, then the planetary supervisor's face appeared on the tiny vidiscreen.

"Good afternoon, Dr. Bones," Simmons said. "You're confirming dinner tonight?"

"Dinner?" Suddenly Zeke recalled that the planetary supervisor had asked him and his friends to his house that evening. "Right, we'll be there. No, actually, I'm calling to ask you to loan me a few men and robots for the afternoon—I want to move some rather heavy artifacts, and will need some help getting them from the tunnels."

"Certainly. I'll send a few down immediately. Will four men and two cargo-handler robots suffice?"

"Perfectly," Zeke said. "Thanks. Oh—we've found a few more of the dragon statues now. I knew you'd be interested."

"Terrific, terrific!" Simmons said. "I'll want to hear all about it at dinner. Eight o'clock sharp!"

"We'll be there," Bones said. "Thanks."

After he'd put the communicator away, he wrote himself a quick note about dinner with Simmons. Then he heard a jumpcar landing outside, and went out to see about the help Simmons had sent—he wanted to get the artifacts safely put away that night.

Jackson met him in the tunnel mouth. "The miners and robots you wanted are here," he said. "Why don't you take a break and have lunch? I can start moving things out."

"Don't let them move anything that isn't labelled for location yet," he said. "I put down the gridwork, but not everything is marked."

"Will do."

Zeke laughed. "Okay, you know the drill. Just make certain they do, too."

And, as he headed for the ramp to the top of the pit, he heard Jackson giving the orders: Bring the artifacts he pointed out to the jumpcar, load them inside—carefully! Wrap the pieces in blankets to make sure they don't break—and fly them up to the storage sheds, where he would show them how to unload.

Zeke paused at the top of the pit and looked down. The miners and the robots had begun bringing the artifacts out, one by one. He watched as two of the humans levered a dragon statue into the jumpcar's cargo hold. They were moving slowly, taking laborious pains not to damage it. *Good*, he thought. *All workmen should be like that.*

As he watched, they covered the statue with a tarp of some kind. When they headed back for the tunnel, Zeke Bones nodded to himself and continued toward the excavation's camp.

Across the mining pit, on the top rim, sat two men. They appeared to be watching the excavation below. *Probably miners*, he thought.

He waved to them, but they appeared not to notice.

"I don't understand," Siona said. "How can you tell their hands had that shape?"

Marty Szigmond sighed to himself and held up the little pole again. He said, in his most patient voice, "The pole has two handgrips, right?"

"Right," Siona said cautiously.

"When you look at the handgrip, you see little indentations for your fingers—all six of them, if you're a Komakoan. See? Count the places for fingers."

Siona did so, and brightened noticeably when she came up with six. "And just from that you can tell what their hands looked like?"

"Working backwards, yes. I have to make a few assumptions, such as the spear-poles were held tightly, and that their grips were comfortable to them. See what I mean?"

"Yes," Siona said. "You're so smart. I never would have been able to figure all that out."

Marty grinned happily. Yes, all in all, things were going better than he ever would have guessed. With Siona along, this promised to be one of the best expeditions he'd ever been on.

He fingered the spear-pole and tried to imagine a creature capable of holding it . . . a dragon, he thought, just like the statues—but with fingers and a brain nearly equal to a human's.

Early evening, in the grasslands east of the mining camp: With the sky darkening and shadows lengthening around them, it was the perfect time for criminals to meet. Or so Felix Alonzo thought, as he sat down and waited for Killian to show up. His back was to their cache—a cave, overgrown by native grass. Wagner had brought down enough stimtabs and Quick and other, more exotic drugs to last through the next six months.

It didn't take long for Killian to arrive. Alonzo heard feet crunching through the alien grass and looked over his shoulder.

"I'm here," Killian said, sitting beside him. "What's wrong?"

"Nothing's wrong—couldn't be better. You heard about Bones and his people finding more artifacts today?"

Killian nodded. "More statues, stuff like that. Yeah, I heard. Why?"

"We're going to take it."

Killian didn't betray a bit of emotion. He just asked, "How?"

"They're all having dinner tonight with Simmons. You will take a jumpcar into their camp, load it with everything you can find, and bring it back here. Clay and I will pack it for vacuum and put it in Wagner's shuttle. When he leaves tomorrow, he'll just take it with him. Neat, efficient, and thoroughly profitable."

"It might work. But what about Bones?"

"Let *me* worry about him. I have something planned that will keep him too busy to worry about a few missing artifacts."

"Does it involve the miners?"

Alonzo smiled. "You know me too well."

"It's not hard to see you've been steering them toward something. How many have we killed now? Six?"

"Not us," Alonzo said, grinning. "It was the 'saurians.' Just ask anyone."

Chapter Nine

Killian moved like a shadow in the dark. He wore black from head to heel, and he'd used black grease paint to cover the paleness of his face.

Two tabs of Quick had heightened his every sense until the world buzzed around him. Air knifed his lungs when he breathed and the night crackled with distant noise: wind in the grass, miners in their little town, the cleanup crew in the pits finishing up the last of the day's work and heading home for the night. Even the shadows stood etched with razor sharpness. He paused, trembling all over, smelling the breeze. He was in tune with Komako, knew every breath the planet took, perceived every hill and every valley, every nook and every cranny within his line of sight. He was the ultimate thief.

He gave the cargo sled's computer its instructions, and it rose silently on a cushion of air, hovering a foot above the ground. When he started for Bones's camp, it followed ten feet behind.

The feast was going well, the last Knight thought. His King and his King's court had gathered at his table, and they all looked well sated; the meal had been a complete success. Even Wagner seemed contented. The *Constellation*'s captain had been on his best behavior, subdued and even a bit witty. His stories of leaves on various planets had certainly done much to lighten the evening's mood.

So Simmons smiled, pleased with himself. It couldn't have gone better. The food had been superb, the conversation memorable, and all had proclaimed their contentment. And as long as Bones was happy, *he* was happy. Keeping Dr. Ezekiel Bones satisfied had become just about the most important thing in his world right now.

"How goes your dig?" he asked finally, feigning interest. It was the one topic that hadn't been covered yet.

"Fairly well," the King said. "You know we opened up several new rooms this morning. More statues were inside, and enough other artifacts to keep researchers busy for years piecing together details of the aboriginals and their civilization."

The robochef began trundling in dessert: dishes heaped with creamy puff pastries. Simmons helped himself, and the robochef moved on along the table. This was his banquet, in his castle, and of course it served him first.

"What of the statues?" Simmons said. "At one point you said you'd come specifically because of them. Were these different than the others? Did they have scales and claws this time?"

The King laughed and said, "I'm afraid not. They were almost exactly the same as the two you'd found, so that mystery remains. Now that we're well into the cataloging process, we've started to make some interesting discoveries. Did you know that the aboriginals seem to have had *two* opposable thumbs on each hand? It leads to some fascinating hypotheses about what they must have looked like."

"You have no idea yet?"

Bones shook his head. "Marty has been working backwards from the handgrip tools we found—the spears

I showed you several days ago, and several others we've just turned up. He's done quite a fascinating reconstruction—though finding a skeleton would certainly make things much simpler!"

"What do their hands look like?"

"Not at all human. They appear to have had overdeveloped talons or claws of some kind, plus four knuckles which may have been double-jointed. Marty has done quite a few preliminary sketches."

"I'd love to see them," Simmons said sincerely. *Two* opposable thumbs? He felt an actual stir of interest this time.

"Meal's over," Marty said, licking the last bit of whipped cream from his fingers. "I could run back and get the sketchbooks, Zeke."

Simmons raised his hands. "No, no, that's too much trouble. I couldn't ask you to do that."

"It's no trouble," Zeke said. "We're always glad when someone's interested in our work. Most people are bored by the routine of archaeology. But this is the exciting part—uncovering an alien civilization piece by piece, putting their lives together like an enormous jigsaw puzzle!"

"Our jumpcar's out front," Jackson said. "I could fly back with Marty, keep him company while he gets the pictures."

Simmons said, "If you're sure you don't mind?"

"Not at all," Jackson said, rising.

Marty winked at Siona. "Be back in a minute."

Safety lamps cast a pale yellow glow over the excavation's camp, but Killian knew he was safe; Bones and his friends were busy fattening themselves with Simmons, and nobody would be guarding the artifacts they'd taken from the tunnels. As Alonzo had said, they'd never have a better chance to grab the stuff and get away with it, especially with Wagner about to leave. If their luck held, the *Constellation* would be out of orbit before Bones even noticed the stuff had been rooked.

Calmly, precisely, knowing that everything would go exactly as planned—exactly as *everything* the boss did went as planned—Killian crept to the main storage shed. The latch clicked open for him. It hadn't even been locked. A conceit on the part of Bones, he thought. With so few people on the planet, with everyone knowing the artifacts were here and nobody having the slightest interest in them, who would have the balls to break in?

He chuckled. *Almost too easy.*

The inside lights came on automatically when he stepped in, and he blinked in surprise as he saw shelves packed with row upon row of Komakoan artifacts, each carefully labelled as to the location it had come from (all in some bizarre notation he couldn't quite follow), what had been found around it, and what holograph would have a picture of it *in situ*.

Most of the artifacts seemed broken in some way; Bones had taken everything, regardless of condition. *Greed*, Killian thought smugly. *Bastard had to have them all.*

Fortunately, there were plenty of unbroken ones to choose from: four more dragon sculptures—a real prize, especially since every one seemed complete. And there were more of the long, thin sticks with tapering points that Alonzo had called spear-poles, plus all the small carved bits of blue stone that he had come to associate with the aboriginals: cubes, intricate geometric plastic weavings, glass tubes that seemed to serve no purpose, and all manner of other things he'd never seen before.

He'd take the large ones first, he decided. Alonzo claimed they'd bring the most money, and money was what Killian wanted most.

He whistled twice into the transmitter at his throat, and his cargo sled glided up to the door. Quickly he hefted the first statue and lugged it over to the sled. It was heavier than he'd thought, and he grunted as he heaved it up into place. Once in the sled's cargo hold, he covered it with a plastic sheet, no use taking chances on chipping it. Then he went back for the next.

He chose another statue. There was more than enough in this little room, he thought, hefting the statue by its wings, to pay his company salary for the next fifty years. He grinned. When they were through on Komako, they'd all be rich men.

It took half an hour to get all the big pieces out and onto the sled. Then he started on the smaller ones, the spear-poles, the colored cubes, the small feathery glass tubes whose purpose he could never fathom.

When the sled was nearly full, he heard a noise that bothered him. The tabs of Quick made him prematurally aware. He paused, straining to hear. A low, distant thrumming noise carried on the wind.

Jumpcar, he thought, fear jangling through him. *Heading this way.*

Bones must have finished early, he thought angrily. Quickly he whistled the sled away, and it floated off toward the cache. Clay and Alonzo would take care of it. He had more important things to worry about.

If he'd only had a few more minutes, Killian thought, he would've finished loading the sled and been able to let it carry him out, too. Now, though, he had to stay and make sure nobody in the jumpcar had seen it—that nobody would follow it. The biggest problem with cargo sleds was their speed. A man in good shape on foot might be able to keep up with one, if he pushed himself. With a jumpcar . . .

Killian decided to act as diversion—he'd attract Bones's attention, make sure they chased him, instead of his sled. Quickly, he eased back into the storage shed. He shut the door and the light went off.

A handful of heartbeats later, he heard the jumpcar land. Doors hissed open; people got out, talking, but the Quick he'd taken jacked their voices into an incomprehensible roar.

Killian counted to three, then banged the door open. The light came on behind him. He paused, silhouetted, and took in the whole of the excavation's camp in one glance.

Two figures stood next to the jumpcar, the tall black man—Bones's assistant—the other the silver-skinned dwarf. The two gaped at him.

He let them look for a good two seconds; that was enough. He let the shed's door slam shut behind him. *Darkness.*

"Hey!" the tall man shouted. "What do you think you're doing there?"

Killian turned and sprinted into the night. The world blurred around him. Hyped on Quick as he was, he knew they'd never catch him, not in the dark, not even with their jumpcar. He grinned. He tucked down his head. He *ran.*

Behind him, he heard the big man giving chase, and the little one shouting into a pocket radio for help. Not that it would do them any good *now*—

When Jackson saw the man in black turn and bolt, his reaction was instantaneous: "Call Zeke," he told Marty, then he launched himself after the fellow.

His legs pumped; he breathed deeply. He moved as fast as he'd ever moved in his life.

But even so, the mystery man was faster. He sprinted up the hill, and Jackson followed, trying to match him stride for stride—and slowly falling behind.

Then the man turned and headed downhill, toward the ramp leading into the north mining pit, and Jackson followed at breakneck speed. *Never give up*, he told himself.

It was dark, but his artificial eye's vision tipped over well into the infrared, and he had no trouble picking out the prowler—his body a hot red against the cooler gray of the alien grass.

The man went down the pit's ramp without slowing, and Jackson didn't let up his own pace for a second. When they hit the pit's floor and the man tucked down his head and ran even faster, pulling away sprinting like a gazelle. Jackson growled to himself and tried to match the other's steps. Centimeter by centimeter, though, he still fell behind.

Gotta be on something, Jackson thought. *Nobody should move like that.*

Then they reached the boulder field at the far side of the pit. The man ducked behind a house-sized boulder, and Jackson lost sight of him.

That brought him up short. No telling what the man had back there—maybe a gun, maybe a knife, and maybe something worse. No sense in walking into a trap; his years as a fighter in the deathpits had taught him that. If you wanted to take someone out, you played by your own rules, not his.

He forced his breathing to slow. While his heart hammered in his chest and blood roared in his ears, he detached a servo from his collar and activated it. It hummed ever so faintly, a little silver-and-plastic dragonfly waiting for instructions. When he stroked one finger along the sleek line of its back, its tiny wings fluttered, lifting it into the air.

"Seek," Jackson whispered, and pointed it in the right direction.

It fluttered toward the boulders, heading up, its little sensors probing the darkness for any movement.

Jackson closed his left eye and activated its remote pickup. A millisecond later, he saw, through the servo's tiny lens, a grainy picture of the ground below.

But it was enough. The man he'd chased was climbing one of the boulders, trying to get away. Jackson hadn't been walking into an ambush after all.

That was enough to get him moving. He opened his eye and flicked his vision back to normal. Time enough to retrieve the servo later—he had a prowler to catch first.

Softly, he cat-footed to the large boulder and inched his way around it. There he listened for half a second, then stole forward to the next.

Seconds later, he heard a scrambling noise to his right. He whirled—and something dark and clinging dropped on him from above.

He fought with it for a second, and panicked when he couldn't move his arms. *Tanglenet*, something in him cried, but by then it was too late—he'd already started struggling, and as the little forcebands contracted about his arms and chest and head, he felt the breath being slowly squeezed from his body.

He gasped, the world around him shimmering and moving. *Relax!* he ordered himself. That was the only way to escape a tanglenet—it responded to all movements by tightening itself.

Jackson tried to draw a breath, couldn't, felt as much as *saw* the darkness creeping around the edges of his vision. He fell, struggling wildly, instinctively, unable to stop himself. The tanglenet squeezed harder—

Suddenly a man loomed before him—a man dressed all in black, laughing crazily as he lifted a huge stone in one hand.

Jackson gasped. *Pain*—

Then darkness took him.

The communicator at Zeke's belt beeped softly. He flipped back the vidiscreen and saw Marty standing in front of the storage shed. "Did you find the sketchbook?" he asked.

"Never mind that," Marty said. "There's been some trouble. Better get back here fast, Zeke."

"What kind of trouble?"

"I'll tell you when you get here. *Hurry*." The viewscreen went dark.

Zeke rose. Sylvie and Simmons were both looking at him curiously.

"I'm afraid you'll have to excuse us," Zeke said to the planetary supervisor. "Marty and Jackson seem to be having some problems back at camp. We'd better get back and see if we can help."

"Nothing serious, I hope."

"I doubt it. I'll have someone drop off copies of the sketches tomorrow. I hope you don't mind."

Simmons just nodded and gestured vaguely. "Quite all right. I'm feeling a bit tired myself, and an early turn-in might be just the thing I need." He smiled at Siona. "I'm afraid that cream puff recipe is going to have to wait till tomorrow."

"That's plenty of time," Siona said. "Thank you."

Bones started for the door. Siona and Sylvie followed on his heels; they seemed to sense the urgency about him. Marty would never call without reason. And why wouldn't he talk in front of Simmons?

"Perhaps," Reelys whispered, "the planetary supervisor would loan us his jumpcar."

"Oh, certainly," Simmons called. He fished in his pocket and pulled out an ignition block. "It's parked around behind the house."

Zeke looked at the shri questioningly.

"It's late," Reelys said. "If there's a problem and you are needed quickly—"

"Thanks," Zeke said, "you're right." He took the cube and said to Simmons, "I'll get it back to you as soon as I can.

"Reelys? Ladies? Let's go!"

Jackson woke slowly. It wasn't till he opened his eyes and tried to sit up that the pain hit him, a wave of it that seemed to radiate from the side of his head. He groaned and pressed his eyes shut.

Slowly, he climbed to his knees. When he touched the side of his head, he found a large bump, swollen and tender, and his fingers came away sticky: blood. Then he recalled, dimly, as though from a dream, the man in black lifting the stone.

Bastard probably hit me with it.

His artificial eye shifted spectrum to infrared and gave him a startlingly clear picture: He lay in the mining pit, still surrounded by boulders big as houses. Only he now had no doubt that he was completely alone.

At least he didn't kill me. He could've done that. Even so, Jackson didn't feel very grateful.

His belt communicator was buzzing incessantly. He finally pawed it free and fumbled back the vidiscreen. It came to light, showing Marty's anxious face.

"Yeah?" he mumbled.

"Jackson, you big lunk! What happened to you? I've been trying for fifteen minutes to get you!"

"The prowler outran me, then jumped me when I wasn't looking."

"When you took off after that creep and I couldn't reach you—"

Jackson sighed. "I'm afraid he dropped a tanglenet on me, then bashed my head with a stone." He glanced around. "No sign of him now, of course. You called Zeke?"

"Ten minutes ago. He's on his way—he got Simmons's jumpcar. Wait, I hear him now."

"Tell him not to rush. I'm all right, and there's nothing we can use to track down that man till morning. I'm heading back. Be there as fast as I can."

"Right."

Jackson clipped the con back at his belt, then stood dizzily and cursed his own clumsiness. *You're getting old, boy*, he told himself. *Slowing down.* Ten years ago, he thought, he would've caught that man and beat him to a bloody pulp before they'd gotten ten feet from the storage shed, no matter what he'd hyped himself on.

Feeling his age, Jackson limped back toward camp.

The call came right on schedule. Felix Alonzo motioned Killian and Clay to silence, took a quick glance around Wagner's shuttle, and decided it was safe to answer. They had been loading the shuttle with vacuum cases from his jumpcar—cases which contained the bulk of the artifacts taken from the storage shed.

Alonzo pushed the voice-only button. The vidiscreen lit up, showing him Simmons's face: The communicator would receive video signals, but not broadcast them.

"Alonzo here, sir," he said.

The planetary supervisor cleared his throat; he didn't look happy. "I'm afraid there's been trouble at Bones's camp."

"What sort of trouble?" Alonzo made sounds of stifling a yawn. "Can't this wait until morning, sir?"

"No, this can't wait until morning! Someone has broken into Bones's storage building and stolen all his artifacts. I don't want word of this to get out—but Bones thinks it may have been some of the miners."

"I hardly think that's too likely."

"Neither do I. But unlikelier things have happened."

"What about the saurians?" Alonzo said. "They could have done it."

"Damn it, there *are* no saurians! All the reports say so. I don't know who could have done it—or even *why*—but I want you to take a walk through the miners' camp immediately. Look for anything unusual. You can investigate more fully tomorrow morning."

"Yes, sir," Alonzo said, letting a note of sullen resignation creep into his voice.

Simmons smiled and hung up on him.

"What now?" Killian asked.

Alonzo laughed. "I get to take a walk through our miners' camp, of course. You two finish here." He picked up the pair of saurian spear-poles he'd set beside the jumpcar. "I'll just need these two little tools, and I'll be all set."

"Have fun," Killian said.

"Oh, I will!" Alonzo laughed again. "I've always fancied myself an unholy terror."

"Why would they want to steal the artifacts?" Zeke wondered aloud, as he sprayed plastiflesh over Jackson's cuts.

Since he'd learned of the theft, he'd run the full gamut of emotions—shock, then disbelief, then raging anger. Now came acceptance . . . and thoughts of how to find the missing artifacts, and quickly, before they were damaged or lost for good.

Jackson bore his pain without flinching. He could have been a brick wall, but Zeke knew it was mostly an act, part of the showmanship he'd learned as a fighter in the deathpits on his home world.

"You gotta duck when people try to hit you, Jackson! Haven't I told you that?" Marty said.

"You'd teach your grandmother to suck eggs, wouldn't you?" Jackson growled back.

"Enough!" Zeke said. "We have more important things to worry about than that!"

"Sorry," Jackson mumbled.

"Me, too," Marty said. "But I can't always be there to watch over you guys."

"Why would anyone steal artifacts?" Siona asked.

"Perhaps someone here wants to get back at you, Zeke," Sylvie said. "You *did* shut down the mining pits. We may find everything dumped in the rock-cruncher tomorrow."

Jackson shook his head, then winced. "They went to too much trouble for that. If someone wanted to inconvenience us, all he'd have to do is use a pick or an axe. This was something more—something organized, something well planned out. That man had a tanglenet, and that's certainly not standard mining camp equipment."

"Actually, it probably would be standard equipment," Zeke said. "In case of riots."

"There is," Reelys said, "one more thing you haven't yet thought of."

"What's that?" Zeke said.

"The black market."

Zeke froze, horrified by the thought. Memories of his father's collection of fabulous artifacts stolen and smuggled to Earth from planets throughout the galaxy leapt unbidden to him: the Galian gyroform clay tablets it was forbidden to remove from their home world, with their curious, undeciphered hyroglyphs; oddly corroded zinc sculptures from the !xaka! home world, though it was illegal for any human to own them; even Fleien temple carvings were there, the most sacred objects from that planet's culture. Had the Fleiens known a human had stolen temple carvings, there might well have been—doubtless *would* have been—attacks on the human bases on Fleia.

Zeke had discovered his father's secret trove by accident, and the shock and horror—and yes, even humiliation—he'd felt had been much of what had decided his future path: following his mother's steps and turning his adult attentions to preserving other cultures instead of plundering them.

Black marketeers disgusted him, especially those who dealt in stolen antiquities. Didn't they realize they were robbing the whole galaxy of valuable cultural heritages? Didn't they know they were violating religious convictions held as deeply as any ever held on Earth? And—beyond that, even—didn't they know they were defying the rules and customs of civilized society?

Finally, though, he managed to control his thoughts. He'd run into black marketeers before, but somehow this time, on Komako, he had his doubts.

When he thought about it, it actually didn't make much sense for black marketeers to swoop down out of nowhere, rob his storage shed, and make off with everything.

"No," he said, "I don't see how it could be the black market this time. Certainly they'd be interested in the artifacts if they could get them—but how would someone smuggle them off the planet?"

"There is a freighter in orbit . . ." Reelys whistled.

"An *ore* freighter, almost completely automated. And don't forget Bill Wagner was with us tonight, and he's the only crewman."

"Perhaps you are right, Ezekiel. Perhaps one or more of the miners are involved. Perhaps they resent our presence, and we have been fortunate up to this point in that nothing has happened. Now we must certainly turn our attentions to the future. Our first concern must be recovering the artifacts."

"But how?" Zeke rose and began to pace. He'd been doing that a lot this last half hour, trying to expend his nervous energy.

"We'll search their camp," Marty said. "They can't have hidden it all in such a small place!"

"Best let Simmons take care of that," Sylvie said.

Zeke nodded. He'd called the planetary supervisor as soon as he'd learned of the theft, and Simmons had promised to have his men look for the stolen artifacts in the morning—nothing could really be done about it at this hour, after all. Which was unfortunate, because a lot could be done with those artifacts in the space of a night.

"Tomorrow I will fly over the camp and look for any traces of the artifacts or those who stole them," Reelys said softly.

"Good idea," Zeke said. "You're probably best qualified for that."

"And you," Jackson said, rising, "should go to bed now."

"I wouldn't be able to sleep."

"You say that on every excavation," he said, smiling a bit for the first time since the theft. "This time we're ready. Reelys brought a complete medical kit just for you—including sleeping pills."

Reelys said, "You know stress does your stomach no good, Ezekiel. You must sleep to keep up your strength."

"That's right, Zeke," Marty said. "You need to take it easier. Don't worry, I'll stay out here and guard the camp."

Siona took Marty's arm. "I'll keep you company," she said. "I wouldn't want you to get lonely."

"It seems I'm outnumbered," Zeke said, looking from one earnest face to another. "All right, but I'm going to be up bright and early tomorrow morning, and I'll expect the rest of you there, too. I'm not about to let those artifacts just disappear."

"That's the spirit!" Jackson said. "We *will* get them back. And I have a score to settle with our thief."

Chapter Ten

Simmons had never made a practice of posting guards around the equipment depots; with the population so small, and the miners so happy, he'd never had a reason to. Alonzo reflected on that as he headed for the transport sleds. These were larger, more powerful models of the cargo sled, used to carry miners to and from the new mining pits.

Alonzo felt grim; he hated wasting good equipment. Fortunately, though, that would be Simmons's problem, not his: the planetary supervisor took ultimate responsibility for everything on Camelot.

The transport sleds sat in a line, sleek and black, just beyond the miners' little town. Twenty meters long and ten wide, they normally carried ore to the smelting station; only recently had three of them been outfitted for humans, with rows of benches bolted to the floor.

He headed for the engine compartment. There he paused, put on gloves, and wiped all marks off the first spear-pole. Only then did he fold back the little panel just in front of the pilot's station.

Inside sat the miniature generator that powered the transport sled. He studied it for a moment, then raised the spearpole, poked the pointed end into the transducer vent, and pushed with all his might.

Something inside the generator snapped; its protective seal broke and the plastic dust-protector slipped to the side. The generator's heart now lay exposed.

With the butt of the spear-pole, Alonzo smashed the tiny memory-wafers that guided the sled. In seconds both the drive and navigation systems lay ruined.

He headed for the second sled, then the third, then the fourth. At the fifth, he worked his sabotage, then broke the spear-pole over his knee. He left it hanging from the open panel.

Turning, he headed back for the miners' camp. There, he activated his communicator and called Simmons. If he wasn't going to get any sleep that night, Alonzo thought, neither would the planetary supervisor.

Simmons answered a moment later, looking bleary-eyed. "What is it?"

"I've been all through the camp, sir. I don't see anything out of the ordinary. Did you want me to look anyplace else, or can I turn in for the night?" *What little's left of it.*

"I can't think of anything else. Get some rest—it's going to be a long day tomorrow."

"Yes, sir," Alonzo said. "Thank you."

The vidiscreen flickered and went dark.

Alonzo hefted the remaining spear-pole and headed home. Killian and Clay would be done by now, and his jumpcar would be back where it belonged. All in all, it had been a very profitable night.

When Zeke woke the next morning, he felt oddly rested and calm. *Something in that sleeping pill Reelys gave me,* he thought.

Rising, he dressed and hurried down to the dining room. All the others were already up and polishing off huge breakfasts. He sat at the head of the table just as the robochef rolled in to set a bowl of something warm and mushy in front of him.

"What's this?" he demanded.

"Oatmeal," Reelys said. "I took the liberty of ordering for you when I heard you getting up. Eat it, Ezekiel. It's good for you."

Zeke sighed and picked up his spoon. It really wasn't bad, he decided after his first bite. He tucked into it with a will, and finished just as everyone else did.

After breakfast they took the jumpcar to the excavation's camp, where the artifacts had been stolen. It looked normal by daylight; the buildings were all in place, the worktables sitting out still covered with notes, the little networked computers untouched.

As soon as they had stepped down from the jumpcar, Reelys began inflating his'er gasbag to full size. Finally s/he floated before them in all his'er splendor, a three-meter-round sphere dangling a fringe of green tentacles. The intricate blue pattern of lines and swirls covering his'er mantle flushed darker than normal—clearly the mission both excited and concerned him'er, Zeke thought.

"Are you sure you want to do this?" he asked the shri, concerned. "I know you're better equipped to look for any traces of a cargo sled than we would be from our jumpcar—but it still might be dangerous."

"I would not have suggested it if I thought there were another alternative," Reelys said. "I am the best equipped to search; therefore, I must go."

"Good luck," Jackson said. He held out a communicator—one of their own special ones from their shuttle, which scrambled the signal between receivers. Reelys took it in his'er tendrils.

"And be careful!" Zeke said. "If you see *anything* that looks the slightest bit dangerous, I want you to come back at once."

"Would you tell a fish to be careful of the water? The air *is* my environment, Ezekiel."

"Point taken," Zeke said. "But the land is our environment, and if any of *us* were going, you'd better believe *we'd* be taking extra care. I mean it! You're too valuable as a friend for me to risk losing you."

"Thank you. I will be careful." S/he started to rise, and finding a southerly air current, drifted off over the mining pit in which Jackson had been ambushed.

Zeke watched him'er go with an uneasy feeling. The shri seemed strangely vulnerable, floating against the mottle of gray clouds—too easy a target to spot, too easy a target to draw a bead on."

"What next?" Jackson asked.

"Hmm?" Zeke looked at his friend. "I want to see our friendly planetary supervisor and see what he has to say about the artifacts being stolen last night."

"Good idea," Marty said. "You know, I always thought he had a criminal face."

"You're so perceptive!" Siona cooed at him.

"You shouldn't leap to conclusions," Zeke said. "But it does strike me as strange that the thieves struck while we were all having dinner at his house. If he knows something, I do intend to find out."

• • •

The human body has its failings and its weaknesses. It is impossible for a normal man under normal conditions to hide a lie from someone who knows what he's looking for—and has the equipment to see it.

From his childhood Zeke Bones had been interested in gadgets of all kinds, and he had been building his own personal servomechanisms as a hobby ever since. He always carried an assortment with him—and they were constantly analyzing the air, the soil, and everything else around him.

They could even serve as crude lie detectors, in a roundabout way. It took but two minutes for him to reset one to measure voice tension and analyze the chemicals in a person's perspiration.

When he was done, he said, "Jackson and I will see Simmons. We should be back soon."

"I'm coming, too," Marty said. "You know you need me, Zeke."

"Actually—" Zeke began.

"You might as well," Jackson said. "He always gets his way."

Zeke sighed. "Did you want to come, too?" he asked Sylvie. "Annoyance in numbers?"

"No—I'm going into the camp itself and have a chat with a few of the off-shift miners. They'll probably know more than Simmons anyway. And I still need a couple of interviews for that documentary."

"You do know how to twist people's arms."

She smiled very sweetly. "Now, what ever do you mean, Dr. Bones?"

He laughed then and looked at Siona. "Someone's got to stay here and keep track of Reelys, in case anything happens to him'er. It's more important than going to see Simmons—do you think you could handle it?"

"Of course," she said primly. "Just show me what to do."

Half an hour later, Bones, Jackson and Marty were shown into Simmons's office by his secretary. Simmons was seated at his desk, a stack of papers in front of him, looking tired and overworked. *He probably didn't get much sleep last night*, Zeke thought. Somehow, he wasn't surprised. Simmons worked hard at his job, and the thefts probably bothered him nearly as much as they bothered Zeke. Disorder in an orderly mining camp was never to be tolerated.

But Simmons put on a serious all-business face, saying, "Good morning, Dr. Bones. I assume you've come about the artifacts." He pushed several pages into a pile and flicked off his computer screen.

"I'll take care of this," Marty said. And before Zeke could stop him, he'd swaggered up to Simmons and said, "I want to know what you did with the statues your men stole from the storage shed last night!"

"Marty!" Zeke said.

"What?" Simmons said after a shocked second, staring at him in confusion. "I resent that question!"

"Please," Zeke started, but Marty pressed on.

"I want to know what you're up to," he said, "and what you plan to do with the statues. You look guilty to me. Take him away, Zeke!"

Simmons said, "I don't know anything about the stolen statues. You were with me when they were stolen!"

"Marty doesn't mean that," Zeke said quickly. The servo he held cupped in his hand told him, from the pheromones Simmons was putting out, plus the stress in his voice, that he really was telling the truth and didn't know a thing about the stolen artifacts.

"I've offered you every hospitality Camelot has to offer," Simmons went on, glowering at Marty, "and what do you do? You accuse me of being a thief. *Me!* A thief! I have better things to do than listen to this. Dr. Bones, if you can't control your people, I will have them removed. *Forceably*, if necessary."

"That won't be necessary," Zeke said. He turned to Marty. "Why don't you wait outside? We'll be through here in a minute."

"Good idea, Doc," he said, still regarding Simmons with suspicion. "I'll see what I can dig up." He headed for the door, calling, "Shout if you need me."

"Unpleasant creature," Simmons muttered, under his breath. Somehow, Zeke couldn't blame him this time: Marty tended to rub people the wrong way.

"Forgive Marty," he said. "He gets a bit carried away at times—but he really does mean well."

"Of course he does."

The servo in his hand bleeped quietly, and Zeke knew Simmons had lied for the first time. Politeness required it, after all.

As Zeke and Jackson settled into the chairs in front of Simmons's desk, the planetary supervisor offered them drinks, which they turned down. Simmons made himself one from the little cart to his right and took a deep swallow. Then he leaned back and seemed to relax.

"That's better," he said, taking another slow sip and savoring the taste. "There's nothing like Sirian brandy."

"Let's get down to business," Zeke said.

"Very well. The things stolen from your storage shed—just statues, was it?"

Zeke shook his head. "Four of the dragon statues, plus nearly a hundred other artifacts. We will have a complete list for you later this afternoon."

"I'll have my men keep a watch out for the statues, but I'm not sure what else I can do. I had my assistant, Felix Alonzo, take a walk through the miners' camp last night, but there was nothing unusual going on."

"What you're saying is there's nothing you can do," Jackson said.

"Essentially, yes. This is a big planet, and I can't see everything that goes on. But there are also very few people here, which makes it easy to limit our suspects to a workable number. And everyone here has been psychoscreened for service with the company—theoretically, none of them should have been able to steal *anything*, let alone break into your camp and make off with that number of artifacts. I want to know what happened, and why, and I'm not going to let my people give up on this matter. Meantime, I can make a few recommendations to you."

"Such as?" Zeke said.

"Keep your storage sheds locked in the future. And let me post a few guards around them."

Jackson said, "Normally we don't have to worry about security—these artifacts shouldn't have been of interest to anyone but us."

"I agree," Simmons said. "But that's clearly not the case here. I really don't understand it. We've never had any such problems before."

"I realize that," Zeke said. "The psychoscreening is what makes the theft so puzzling. And there's nothing anybody could possibly gain from taking the artifacts. How would they get them off-planet without us noticing?"

"Strange indeed," Simmons said. He drained the rest of his drink and leaned over to fix himself another. "Are you sure you don't want one?" he said.

"No, thank you."

"Ah." He took a tentative sip, then nodded to himself. "Well, I don't know what more I can do. As I told you, I personally know nothing about the whole affair, nor do

I have any logical explanation. Will you let me post those guards?"

"Yes," Zeke said. "I'm not happy, but I guess that will have to do for now. Are you sure you don't have any idea who might be responsible?"

Simmons hesitated a fraction of a second, then said, "No."

Zeke's servo bleeped again. His eyes narrowed. *He knows something he isn't telling.* Perhaps it was time to change tactics, he thought.

Abruptly, Zeke leaned forward and set the servo he held onto the edge of Simmons's desk. "Do you know what this is?" he asked.

Simmons studied it: a small gray box that hummed ever so softly to itself. "No."

"A form of lie detector."

"I resent—"

"You seem to be resenting a lot of things," Jackson said.

Zeke went on. "I had to know you were telling me the truth when you said you weren't involved. I meant no offense, but when theft on this scale is committed, I *have* to know whom I can trust. Now, I need those artifacts back, and I intend to find them. I'm a man used to getting my way, Mr. Simmons, as I'm sure you can imagine."

Simmons drew back and regarded Zeke for a long minute over the rim of his glass. "You're one of the most powerful men in the human universe," he said at last, in a cold, quiet voice. "You can break me in an instant if you want to. But I've done a bit of checking on you too, Dr. Bones, and from what I've found out, you're a fair man, as honest as they come. I have done nothing to offend you, nor to obstruct your excavation, even though it's played hell with my schedule. I may not like what you're doing—in fact, if it were up to me, I'd blast those tunnels and everything in them to rubble and run them through the crunchers—but I respect authority. I'm a company man, Dr. Bones, and I try to follow orders. *I'm* going to have to deal with the mess here after you leave. If you push me around, force me to resign or fire me, then things are only going to get worse. There's nobody else qualified to do my job on Komako right now, and it would take six months for a replacement to arrive. Now, why don't you go play storm trooper someplace else and let me handle this? I know my people. I know where to look, and what to look for. How about letting me do my job?"

Now it was Zeke's turn to lean back and think for a moment. Simmons was proving to be quite a complex man. He had seemed too easy to figure out the first time they'd met—the company man driven by a need to do good for his men, striving to please the visiting officials to help his career. Now, with a bit of pressure on him, his apparent flab suddenly showed as muscle. It was obvious why he'd risen so high in the Panadium Trading and Mining Company's ranks.

Zeke finally said, "Perhaps we shouldn't be working at cross purposes. You have more than demonstrated your loyalty to your people and your company, and this servo proved your innocence. I know I can trust you."

"Thank you. I would certainly rather work with you than against you."

Zeke nodded, actually respecting him for the first time. Now that they understood each other, perhaps they could get somewhere. He took the servo off the desk, switched it off, and returned it to his pocket. "Now," he said, "you had a thought about who might be responsible?"

Simmons shifted a bit uncomfortably. "It's crazy, really," he said. "I don't know what made me think about it."

"Try us."

"Well . . ." He licked his lips, then took another sip of brandy. "It's the miners."

"Which ones?"

"All of them. They're poor, uneducated, and very superstitious. Since you got here and started excavating the tunnels, I've been hearing stories . . . I take it you haven't heard them yet? Well, I'm not surprised—you're probably the last ones they'd tell. These stories go like this: You've been poking around in those tunnels, and now things have started to go wrong all around camp. Just this morning five of the transport sleds were vandalized by someone using one of those alien spears. And there has been minor theft all around camp, but the stuff that's missing doesn't make much sense, either: it's nothing valuable, or even personal. It's dinner trays. It's clothing hung out to dry. It's sacks of corn meal. It's—"

"What are you getting at?"

Simmons frowned. "Miners aren't the brightest people in the world. They can't be, or they wouldn't be miners. So they look at things going wrong and they say, 'Everything was fine till Bones got here, so it must be his fault things are going wrong now.' Do you follow me so far?"

Zeke shifted uncomfortably, not liking the direction this story was heading. "Pretty well."

"There are rumors going around the camp that aboriginals still live in the tunnels. They've just been hiding until now . . . sort of a truce or stand-off between us and them. And because you're stirring things up and going through their tunnels stealing their belongings, they're taking it out on the miners."

"That's ridiculous."

"I agree—most rumors are. But they're still real, and they're still something my men and I have to deal with, as I'm sure you understand."

Aboriginals . . . Zeke thought. No, it wasn't possible for any aboriginals to be alive—was it?

The day looked perfect for flying, Reelys thought, as s/he floated over the mining camp. A pleasant breeze buoyed him'er up toward the clouds, but s/he forced him'erself to stay closer to the ground, thoughts firmly focussed on the task at hand.

From above, it was possible to see all sorts of things normally hidden below. First s/he took in the entire expedition's camp, paying particular attention to the storage shed where the artifacts had been kept. S/he guessed the statues had been moved onto a cargo carrier of some kind, and finding evidence of it was his'er first priority.

The green of the alien grass had been disturbed, s/he noted on the far side of the hill. S/he drifted in that direction. Yes—there seemed to be a faint trail, as though repeller fields from a cargo sled had pressed down on the grass and it hadn't quite recovered yet.

That faintest of trails led east, away from the camp, toward a series of small hillocks. The shri manipulated the radio s/he held in his'er tentacles.

"Siona?" s/he said.

"Yes, Reelys?" came the immediate answer.

"I see what may be the sled's trail, heading away from the camp. I am going to follow it."

"Are you sure you wouldn't rather wait for Marty and Zeke to come back?"

"No. The grass is recovering quickly in the daylight. If we wait, the trail might well vanish entirely."

"Then be careful," Siona said.

Reelys found an air current heading in the proper direction and drifted up into it. As s/he followed the pressed-down grass into the hills, s/he grew more and more excited. If someone were going to hide a cargo sled full of artifacts, they'd need a place to get it under cover, and the hills offered the best chance of cover.

The trail wound on. Reelys followed it over a low ridge—and came up short.

There—wasn't that a sled, half-hidden behind a jutting stone? S/he moved closer, descending for a better look.

Metal glinted. The shri focussed his'er attention, and saw something moving in the shadows next to the cargo sled. A man—wasn't that a man?

"Siona!" Reelys called excitedly. "I found them—"

And next instant came a flash of light and a burning sensation, and the weird vertigo a shri gets when his'er airbag has been ruptured. Reelys howled in fear and agony as only a shri can.

"*Help me!*" s/he tried to say, as air whipped around and through him'er. The breeze kited him'er away from the sled and its guardian.

Then the ground swayed violently and seemed to rush up.

Zeke's wrist communicator buzzed. He pushed the button impatiently. "Yes?"

It was Siona, and she sobbed, "Zeke—they've shot Reelys!"

Chapter Eleven

If Sylvie Pharr had learned one thing during all her years as a reporter, it was that people would talk about anything and everything, if you put them in the right situation.

When she walked into the miners' camp, her holocameras floating in a line behind her, she got a number of odd looks from the men and women there, but none of them came up and spoke to her. She might have been some weird alien creature wandering among them, rather than a beautiful woman.

And, she thought, there seemed to be an unusually large number of miners present; shouldn't they be at the new mining pit? Did their presence have something to do with the stolen artifacts?

Finally she came to the company cantina. It was a huge building, typical of a frontier place, completely prefabricated. The outside walls had been designed to look like weathered wood, and the glass-paned windows all had shutters.

She'd been looking for a place like this; a cantina setting would do nicely. And a bit of alcohol could loosen any human's tongue.

She pushed through swinging double doors and found herself in a surprisingly homey main room. Huge woodenlike beams crossed the ceiling, and a huge stone-fronted fireplace dominated the wall to her left. Hanging lights and plants brightened the place, and colorful murals provided a welcome contrast from the greens and grays that dominated the camp. Low, thrumming music piped from hidden speakers.

Directly in front of her stood a long bar with barstools. Glasses hung from racks overhead; behind it, on mirrored shelves, stood row upon row of bottles, more mugs and glasses. Holographic pictures of miners (she assumed they were regulars here) had been taped to many of the shelves, along with travel posters from exotic worlds and all the other bric-a-brac that accumulates over the years.

Perhaps a dozen men and women stood or sat at the bar, and two dozen more reclined at various tables and booths. Sylvie smiled dazzlingly and moved forward.

Slowly the murmur of talk died as she became the center of attention. She reached the bar, seated herself, then swung around to take in the whole of the cantina.

"Good evening, gentlefolk," she said, in a loud, cheerful stage voice. "Some of you may recognize me from the newsvids. My name's Sylvie Pharr, and I'm looking for a few good men—and women."

The usual whistles and catcalls came, but she just smiled and waited. Sex sells, she'd learned long ago; often it got her where mere talent never could.

She winked at the barkeep. He was a tall, thin man, with bushy gray eyebrows and a receding hairline. He wiped his hands on his apron.

"What can I get you, Ms. Pharr?" he asked.

"What's good?"

"Nothing. But none of it'll kill you."

She laughed, and he drank it in. "What about your wine?"

"White?"

"Green."

"Ah, the stuff from Deneb. I think there's a bottle in the back room—" Muttering to himself about his inventory, he went to go see.

"Now—" Sylvie leaned back and crossed her legs, and found all eyes focussed on her. She liked it that way. "How about gathering around and listening to what I have to say? I don't bite . . . often."

Hesitantly, it seemed, they rose and moved forward, circling her, listening but offering no help or support. Their faces remained impassive. She might have been talking to statues, instead of people. *Get on with it,* Sylvie told herself.

She said, "I'm filming a documentary on Dr. Bones's expedition, and I'd like to interview a couple of you for your thoughts about the dragon statues, and the aboriginals, and the planet in general. It won't make the newsvids, of course—but it will be seen in schools throughout the galaxy. Is anyone interested? You'd be doing me a big favor."

The barkeep returned with a dusty bottle in hand, and Sylvie motioned for two glasses. Silently he placed them before her, then uncorked the bottle, and set it there, too. Sylvie poured herself a finger's portion of the bubbly green stuff, took a sip, and nodded at the familiar spicy, mintlike flavor. It left a tingly feeling in her tongue.

Then she scanned the faces of the crowd around her, seeing interest and something else—was it fear?

None of them moved.

Sylvia sighed inwardly, but didn't let her disappointment show. She drained the rest of her drink and poured herself another.

"There's nothing illegal or immoral about talking to me," she said. "I'm here by permission."

"Out of the way, lunks!" bellowed a woman with a low-pitched voice. "Coming through!"

The crowd jostled, and a stout middle-aged woman with short-cropped black hair pushed through to the front. She wore a gray uniform of a miner, and somehow she seemed born to it. Her face had a rough-chiselled quality, and with thick, muscular arms and legs like tree stumps, she looked strong enough to break any man in the place in half. She took a quick look at the miners gathered around, laughed loudly, pushed several back a few feet, and swaggered up to the bar. When she had plunked herself down on the stool next to Sylvie, she grinned and stuck out her hand.

"Name's Rose," she said. "I'll talk to ya, if these rock-heads don't got the sense. Besides, I've got a powerful thirst to try that Deneb stuff."

Sylvie shook hands—Rose's grip was firm, but not overpowering. At last she'd found what she'd come looking for, she thought.

"The wine's a bit spicy," Sylvie said, pouring Rose a glass, "but I think you'll like it."

Rose drained it in one gulp, smiled approvingly, and slapped the countertop. "*Dee*-licious. Now, whatcha wanna know, Ms. Pharr?"

"Call me Sylvie," she said, refilling Rose's glass. "Everyone does. Now, you're sure you don't mind talking? Everyone else seems so reluctant—"

"Nah. I'm a company gal, born and bred, and I can see trouble coming a klick away. You ain't it. Besides, I just renewed my contract for another tenner, and can't nobody take *that* away!" She laughed long and hard.

Sylvie subvocalized her commands to the hovering holocams, and they took up unobtrusive positions over the miners' heads. They began recording.

"Tell me about the tunnels," Sylvie said. "Were you there when they found the first two?"

"Sure. We all were, just 'bout. First that moron Dmitri Wu dragged the statues out, then work stopped as the pit supervisor tried to sort everything out, and the boss himself come down to try to set it all back to runnin'. Not long after that's when the trouble started."

"Trouble?" Sylvie asked, brow wrinkling. Nobody had mentioned trouble among the miners—

"Yeah," Rose said, warming to the subject. She helped herself to more wine this time, and swilled it around her mouth before swallowing. "Now, some of the boys think it's a curse, or bad luck, but I'm not the superstitious type and don't believe it. It's only stuff ya can hold that can hurt ya, y'know?"

"Uh-huh," Sylvie said encouragingly.

"Anyways, it all started 'bout a week or two after them first two tunnels opened up. That's when Dmitri Wu— rest him quiet—got hit by a falling stone. Busted his head wide open, too—you shoulda seen it! Brains everywhere." She chuckled. "Never knew that man had so many."

"Just an accident," Sylvie said. "They happen."

"That's what everybody said. 'Just an accident'—just like that. But it weren't. There've been too many other 'accidents' for just bad luck. Pietr Amadov found the next tunnel, and two nights later he went out for a walk and never came back—search party found him the next day. Said it was a heart attack, but Petey never had nothing wrong with his heart. I seen his med records once."

"So what happened to him?"

"I think they scared him t' death." Rose nodded solemnly, and the crowd began to mutter among itself.

"Who murdered him?"

"The saurians."

The mutters in the room grew to dark rumblings as she said it, but Rose glared at them. "Hush up!" she said. "Can't you see I'm talkin'?"

They hushed up.

"What saurians?" Sylvie said. "Who are they?"

"That's what we've been calling 'em—you know, the dragon-people who live in the tunnels. I figure they've been hiding down there where we can't see 'em or get at 'em. Every time we run into another of their tunnels, something bad happens—revenge, I figure. Y'know?"

"Why didn't Simmons mention that?"

"The supervisors, they all feel the same, 'Bad luck,' they say, 'nothing more,' they say—but the bad things, they keep happenin' just the same, and there's nothing that seems t' stop it."

"Is it always someone getting killed?"

"Nah, mostly it's other stuff. Like two weeks ago, just after you an' Dr. Bones got here, there was the two crushers that got broke up during the night. Someone put danger flares in 'em and they burned right through to the core, y'know? They're in the shop getting repaired still. And this morning they found five of the transport sleds with busted engines—that'll take another week to set straight. That's why we're all here today, 'stead of out working the pits—no way to get us there. It's always stuff like that. No miner would do it—it has t'be someone else. It has t'be the saurians."

"How do you know it isn't a miner? Someone who hates the camp here, and wants it stopped?"

"Lordy, no!" Rose shook her head, looking completely bewildered. "We're all company people here, and we all love this planet—nicest place I ever worked, and since them tunnels been turnin' up, we've all been workin' half-shifts at full pay. This is sure the easiest job *I* ever had, and it's the same for everyone else. Real food, outside work, good pay and bonuses—this is the way minin' planets're supposed to be run. We're all family, y'know? Ain't nobody got reason to complain. *Nobody*."

Sylvie nodded and stood. "I'd like to talk to you again later," she said, "if you don't mind."

"Any time," Rose said.

Sylvie smiled warmly. "Terrific. Why don't you finish the rest of the bottle? I'm sure you have friends who might want to try it."

"Why, thanks!" Rose beamed at her. "I really appreciate that, Sylvie!"

"Enjoy." She smiled and slid off the barstool, starting for the door, holocams floating in a train behind her. She knew Zeke would want to hear about the problems the miners were having—and their suspicions of the saurians—as soon as possible.

Killian shouldered his energy rifle and cursed. He'd come to the smugglers' cache one final time to make sure they hadn't missed anything when they'd emptied it the night before, and he'd just been coming out of the cave when he'd seen the shri heading toward him. Somehow, it had found the cave: It was heading straight down toward him.

Instinctively, he'd aimed and shot. His first bolt hit the shri dead-on, and with a tortured shriek, the creature had whipped across the sky like a punctured balloon, finally falling beyond the hill.

A second later he had realized he'd made a mistake. Alonzo would be furious.

Killian had violated his orders and used an energy weapon instead of one of the saurian spear-poles. Like Alonzo had said, anyone who found the shri would know a human had done it. But it had been instinct, action without thought, pure defense mechanism. Maybe he'd junked himself on too much Quick. Or maybe not enough.

The jumpcar he'd used to get here still sat in the cave, out of sight, next to the cargo sled. He leaped in, started the engine, and headed for the mining pit. Carefully, he kept low, hiding behind the hills, circling around as best he could. It might not be too bad, he decided, so long as nobody knew who'd done it.

Alonzo would set things right, come up with a plan. He always did.

As soon as Siona said Reelys had been shot, Zeke was up and running for the door, Jackson on his heels. Behind, they heard Simmons rising to follow.

Jackson passed Zeke outside the door and was the first one into the jumpcar. He jammed the ignition cube into place and began powering up the engine.

Zeke swung into the passenger compartment, and Simmons followed him in. Jackson took off at a stomach-wrenching acceleration a half-second later. When Zeke looked back, he saw Marty standing in the doorway, staring at them with a bewildered expression on his face. *No chance to tell him*, Zeke thought, with a twinge of guilt. Still, they'd talk to him as soon as they could. In normal circumstances he would have called Marty on his pocket communicator, but now he had more important things to do with it.

"Shot, did she say?" Simmons asked, panting from the run. His face looked pale in the darkness, and his hands trembled noticeably.

"That's right," Zeke said. He opened up his communicator, switched its directional beacon to match Reelys's, and noted with relief that the shri's communicator still worked. He passed it forward, to Jackson.

"Head east," he said.

"Right, Doc."

"We've never had any problems like that before," Simmons was saying. "I don't understand. . . ."

He trailed off, and nobody spoke to fill the silence. Somehow, Zeke didn't feel like talking. Inside, he *knew* he never should have let Reelys go up. It had been too dangerous. If the shri were badly hurt, or even dead, he knew he'd never be able to forgive himself. Then and there he made a vow. He'd find out who had done it, no matter how much it cost, no matter how long it took.

"There," Jackson said. "To the right. I see him'er—s/he's on the ground."

Zeke leaned forward, straining to see. The aircar swung around. Then he spotted the dim smudge on the ground ahead. Jackson's artificial eye had picked it out as the shri before any normal human ever could have.

Jackson accelerated again, closing with the ground. Zeke could hear the alien grass's seedpods hitting the bottom of the jumpcar with little jarring thumps as they skimmed over it.

They neared the shri. Swallowing his nervousness, Zeke popped the side door and leaped out before they had quite stopped.

He ran to Reelys's side and knelt. The shri made a soft, whispery sound, halfway between sob and whimper.

"Easy, friend," Zeke said softly. "We're here. We'll take care of you now."

Carefully he rolled Reelys over. When he saw the gaping wound, he felt sick to his stomach.

An energy bolt had punched a good twenty-centimeter-round hole through the shri's airbag. Heat had charred its edges black. Zeke knew a shri had to maintain a carefully balanced internal pressure, or would soon lose consciousness and die. He tried to block the hole with his hands, but they weren't large enough to do any good. He cursed in frustration.

Jackson reached him a moment later, lugging the jumpcar's emergency medical kit. He set it down and flipped back its lid.

"We need something to patch his airbag, and fast," Zeke said.

"Tape gauze over it, and spray plastiflesh on the gauze," Simmons said, coming up behind. "That should do for the moment."

"It's worth a try."

Zeke took the gauze. While he unrolled it, Jackson began snipping off bits of sterile tape. Zeke applied both liberally to the wound, covering the hole. He felt air wheezing through the gauze as Reelys struggled to reestablish his'er internal pressure.

Jackson handed him the can of plastiflesh and he began to spray a thick coat around the wound. It solidified into a rubbery coating almost at once. And immediately Reelys's airbag began to puff up. Slowly the shri rose, looking gray and chalky, gray-green tendrils quivering. S/he shifted his'er mantle until the plastiflesh no longer showed, and continued to hover there in silence.

"Will that hold?" Zeke asked.

Reelys made an unintelligible whispery noise, paused a moment, then tried again: "I . . . believe . . . so."

"I don't know all that much about shri physiology. What should I do now?"

"Nothing . . . I . . . must . . . rest. . . ."

"We'll take you back to camp," Jackson said.

"No . . . in the hills . . . there is a cave . . . I can get . . . back . . . to camp. . . ." As if to prove his'er point, Reelys began to drift upwards, and finding a breeze toward the excavation's camp, moved off in that direction.

Zeke watched his friend go with mingled relief and worry. Plastiflesh was strong—but it wasn't designed for use on a shri, and if anything went wrong now, he would never forgive himself.

"We're going to follow him'er back," he said, starting for the jumpcar. "We can get the full story in camp. I don't want to rush into the hills looking for a cave and someone with an energy rifle."

"I'll arm some of my men and have them take a look," Simmons promised. A frown creased his face. "I won't tolerate violence on my planet."

"We can drop you off at your office," Zeke said, "after we make sure that Reelys has made it back to our camp safely."

"Just let me call my camp supervisors," Simmons said. "Rest assured, we'll soon get to the bottom of all this."

What does he want this time? Alonzo thought, as he pushed through the door into Simmons's office.

He'd had less than three hours of sleep the night before, and keeping up his appearance of being the dutiful second-in-command had made him rise at dawn and pretend to investigate the sabotaged transit sleds. Now he felt leaden inside, his eyes cottony and his arms and legs wooden. He really needed to go home and sleep. *At least the bastard finally moved out of my house*, he thought.

Simmons had called him, and when Simmons called, he always came running. Just like the obedient dog Simmons thought he was. *When I'm retired*, he thought, *things will be different.*

"There's been a shooting," Simmons said, as soon as Alonzo closed the door behind himself. "Someone put a hole in Bones's shri."

Alonzo felt a cold shock run through him. "What—how—"

"That's what I want you to find out. The shri's alive, barely. It mentioned something about a cave in the hills. Arm yourself and a few other men you trust and go have a look. and *be careful*—whoever did it showed no hesitation in shooting the shri, and I can't afford to lose any of my men. That includes you."

It must have been Killian, Alonzo thought angrily. *That psychopath! I'm going to have to do something about him—and soon.*

"Yes, sir!" he said to Simmons.

• • •

"Really," Reelys said, "I am feeling much better now, Ezekiel. Remember, I do not quite feel pain as you know it. The part of my body that was shot is already healing, and the only sensation I have there at the moment is numbness."

"Nerve damage?" Sylvie said.

"Certainly," Zeke said, "but the shri can regenerate damaged nerves, much as starfish on Earth regenerate whole limbs. I think s/he's going to be all right."

"Of course I am," Reelys said, sounding a bit peevish. "I just said that."

"I'm glad," Sylvie said. "Oh, Zeke—in the excitement I completely forgot! I found out something very interesting in the miners' camp."

"What's that?" he asked.

"I did an interview with one of the miners, and she said some pretty weird stuff. You're going to have to see it."

She crossed to her bag and removed the holocube her cameras had recorded onto. Activating it, she set it on the worktable before them.

A rainbow of colors shimmered, then the bar appeared, Sylvie seated next to Rose, both of them sipping their wine.

Zeke watched aptly as the mining woman spoke of the sabotage, and her fears about the saurians. And as she spoke, he began to get an uncomfortable feeling in the pit of his stomach.

Later that afternoon, the last Knight of Camelot sat in his office, head cradled in his hands, eyes pressed shut. His head hurt, and not even his brandy could soothe the ache—it came from the mind, rather than the flesh. *Bad news all the way around*, he thought.

Seeing the shri lying on the ground had upset him. It capped a colossally horrible day. First the theft, then the sabotage, then Bones questioning him. At least Wagner had gone, he thought. He'd moved back to his house first thing that morning, and the first thing he'd done was set his robot butler to airing the place out. It stank, like an animal's den.

Simmons's desk communicator shrilled at him suddenly. He punched the button, and the face of his communications officer appeared.

"What now?"

"Sir," he said, "We have a call from Captain Wagner. He wishes to speak with you. He says it's quite important."

"Put him through."

The picture cut to show Wagner, his beard wild, his hair unkempt. Static and double-images ghosted across the screen, somehow magnifying the horror. *At least he's in orbit*, Simmons thought. Over Wagner's shoulder he could see the clutter of the pilot's personal quarters.

Wagner just glared for a minute. "Your men screwed up the engines," he finally snapped, slamming his fist down for emphasis. "The timing sequence is *still* all wrong. How the hell am I supposed to make my schedule if they can't get a simple recalibration right?"

"Are you sure it's not a system's error—"

"I *know* what a system error looks like, and I tell you they screwed up the recalibration! What are you going to do about it?"

Simmons swallowed. "Bring down the shuttle. I'll send the technicians up to work double shifts until it's done right."

"Good," Wagner growled, and switched off his communicator.

Simmons did the same. And a second later the damn thing shrilled again.

He punched the button. "What!"

"Sir?" said Alonzo, looking at him strangely.

"Eh? Sorry. Never mind." Simmons took a deep breath. *A knight is always calm, always fair.* "What is it? Did you find the cave?"

"Yes, sir. We found the cave, and it has one of our cargo sleds in it, but that's all. Not a sign of anybody. Oh, and this cave . . . it appears to be the entrance to still more aboriginal tunnels. Perhaps the saurians—or who-ever shot the shri—went in deeper. Do you want us to follow?"

"Negative, don't do that," Simmons said. "Bones wouldn't like it. Leave two men there to guard it, and set up a series of shifts so they can be relieved. I don't want anything getting into—or out of—that cave without my knowing it."

"Yes, sir," Alonzo said. "I'll bring the cargo sled back."

"Do that. Then report here. I have some other prob-lems I'll need your help with."

"Immediately, sir."

The last Knight leaned back and closed his eyes, trying to think of something pleasant. Nothing came to mind. It really had been a horrible day, and it had scarcely begun.

Finally, though, he knew he had work to do. Duty always kept him going. That and his fantasies of chivalry. He had to get those techs back to Wagner's ship, and he had to tell Bones what Alonzo had found. Neither task appealed to him.

More tunnels. He shuddered. *Just what I need right now.*

And he began to wonder if the stories of aboriginals still being alive might not be true.

Chapter Twelve

Zeke switched off his communicator thoughtfully. Carter Simmons had just told him what Alonzo had found, and the thought of another series of tunnels—these with their own entrance to the surface—gave him pause. If there were I aboriginals still alive and hiding, they'd have to be in places like that. But still . . . something didn't quite ring true to him.

He wandered back to the worktable where the others sat. Quickly he sketched out what Alonzo had found.

"What do you think?" he asked.

"It's a frame job," Marty announced. "It's obvious there are no so-called 'saurians' here."

Jackson agreed. "Someone wants us to believe there are, though," he said. "No saurians would have stolen a cargo sled—or have shot Reelys with a *human* energy rifle."

"The saurians wouldn't have been able to shoot a rifle accurately even if they somehow managed to steal one," Marty said. "Remember those sketches I made of their hands?" He dug one out of the stack of papers on the table and waved it around. "Look at how thick and blunt their fingers are. They're perfect for holding spear-poles, but human-sized guns? Never."

"So that's it," Zeke said slowly. "It all comes back to humans in the end. But who—and most of all, *why?*"

"Let us start at the beginning," Reelys said. "You must eliminate the impossible, as one of your planet's great thinkers said, and whatever is left, no matter how improbable, will be the truth. Start by proving for Mr. Simmons and his miners that these saurians are extinct. That will stop the rumors and allow all of us to focus our attentions in the right direction."

"What do you suggest?" Zeke said.

"The aboriginal tunnels we explored so far have all proved long-empty. Doubtless the rooms in the cave will be the same. So you must set up cameras at each of the openings and have them monitored at all times. It would also be a good idea to run analyses on the animal life in the sea."

"Why do that?" Marty said. "Talk about distractions!"

Reelys said, "Perhaps the oddest thing about this planet is its lack of land animals. As the aboriginal artifacts demonstrate, this was not always so. I find the puzzle most perplexing. Perhaps the answer to this mystery lies in the sea. I believe the reports Zeke has on this planet mention its abundant ocean life."

"Getting samples shouldn't be a problem," Jackson said. "I can take one of the jumpcars down to the beach and see what sort of fish I can catch. It's been a long time, but I used to be quite a good fisherman."

"Good idea," Zeke said. "You can take Marty with you."

"And Siona," Marty said quickly.

Siona said, "We can make it into a picnic!"

Sylvie smiled at Zeke. "Why don't we go, too? You said this was going to be a vacation, and you certainly haven't been relaxing."

"When do I have time to relax—especially with all that's going on!"

"Time away from the stress of this excavation would do you good, Ezekiel," Reelys said. "As your physician, I recommend it."

He had to laugh at that. "I guess I haven't been taking things as slowly as I should be. And I imagine we could all use a break. You've talked me into it—we can make an expedition of it tomorrow. What about you, Reelys? Everyone else wants to come."

The shri whistled plaintively. "I am afraid I must pass. I have no love for water—and water in such quantities I find more than a bit daunting. Instead, I will stay here and watch over the remaining artifacts. And the tunnels, when you get the cameras in place."

"And you need time to heal," Zeke said.

"Yes. Quite."

"I'll get the equipment we'll need from the *Heinrich Schliemann*," Jackson said.

Two hours later, Zeke and Sylvie had finished setting up the cameras in the mining pits and headed for the cave. It was easy to spot from the air: A two-seater jump-car sat atop the nearby hill, and two men in gray uniforms sat in its shade, looking down on the cave's mouth.

The two scrambled to their feet as Zeke landed his jumpcar. He couldn't help but notice the heavy-duty energy rifles they wore slung over their shoulders. Simmons obviously wasn't taking any chances.

"I hope you realize this isn't going to help my documentary," Sylvie said. She'd volunteered her holo-cams as the surveillance devices, and now only one remained—the one they'd set up to monitor the cave's entrance.

"Oh, I doubt if you'll miss terribly much. You'll have more of a story if the saurians *do* show up. If they do, we'll have a recording of them."

"Only two-dimensional."

"That's served well enough in the past. Reporters didn't always have holocams, you know!"

"Let's just get done and get out of here." She picked up her last holocam, almost reluctantly, it seemed to Zeke. He knew she had other, more subtle recording devices, so he didn't feel that badly about depriving her.

The two guards made no attempt to approach—probably had orders only to let Bones and his people near the cave—so Zeke and Sylvie headed down the hill toward the entrance.

The clumps of grass that once overhung the opening had all been stripped away, exposing the whole of the cave entrance. It had squared-off sides and a rounded ceiling, much like the aboriginal tunnels in the mining pits. The stone here looked different, though, Zeke thought—sedimentary, rather than igneous.

Disturbed, he took the light from his belt, flicked it on, and went in. "I'll be back in a moment," he called over his shoulder.

Inside, he paused to let his eyes grow accustomed to the dimness. A few broken artifacts lay on the floor: a pair of spear-poles, their shafts shattered; a few broken cubes; a few bits of yellow glass that might have come from one of the thin yellow tubes they'd found.

Zeke ignored the artifacts. The place had about the right dimensions for an aboriginal tunnel, he thought, but something felt different about it, oddly sterile, like a museum recreation rather than an original scene.

He turned to study the walls. They were polished smooth, too smooth, as though done by machinery. And the floor was sand rather than stone; it crunched under his feet as he moved. Kneeling, he brushed it aside, digging as deeply as he could. Finally he touched stone about fifteen centimeters down. Quickly, he began clearing a space on the floor.

A few dark spots of oil remained. He didn't have to check his servos to know this cave had been man-made, merely disguised to look as though inhabited by the aborigines recently.

He poked into the next two rooms, which ended in deadends. The place had been carved out of the rock. No tunnels stretched further into the hills. And no aboriginal had ever been inside, of that he was certain.

He emerged just as Sylvie finished setting up the holo-cam. It stood on a small tripod, lens pointed at the cave's mouth. Nothing would be able to get in or out, day or night, without her camera picking it up and beaming the picture back to their receiving station.

She activated the camera and stood back, regarding it critically. "That ought to do," she said, giving it an affectionate pat.

"How about it, guys?" Zeke said to his communicator. "Marty?"

"The picture's coming through adequately," Marty said. "It will do."

"Great," Zeke said, grinning at Sylvie. "Since the tunnel's man-made, I doubt we'll have much excitement here."

"Man-made?" Sylvie said.

Zeke nodded. "Yep, and I bet I know where the equipment came from."

"The miners!"

"That's right. Let's get back to camp. I still have to fill Simmons in on our plan. I just hope we don't catch any saurians in the meantime—I don't think Reelys could stand being wrong."

In the mining camp, Felix Alonzo had just finished moving back into his house. With Bill Wagner already in orbit in his ship, everything had begun returning to normal. He was glad to be rid of the pilot—and glad the cargo of artifacts had been shipped out. Now he could get back to the routine of their operations.

He settled onto his sofa, leaned back, and closed his eyes. Just as he'd begun to doze off, a pounding started on his door.

"It's me!" he heard Killian call. "Open up! I have to talk to you."

Sighing, Alonzo sat up and motioned for his robot butler to let Killian in. The thing floated over and opened the door.

Killian stormed it, babbling about energy rifles and flying shri.

"Wait a minute!" Alonzo said. "Slow down. Start from the beginning."

Killian took a deep breath, then slowly and simply told what had happened at the cave. Alonzo kept nodding encouragingly. Finally, five minutes later, he had the whole story straight.

And, when he did, he didn't like it. He stood and began pacing, all thoughts of sleep gone.

"You may have screwed up everything," he said. "You're sure you saw them setting up cameras today to watch the tunnels?"

"That's right," Killian said gloomily. "They're everywhere. I heard the cameras are supposed to prove there aren't any saurians. They've told everyone that. And with all the evidence they have, people are starting to believe it."

"That's rather clever of them. Almost worthy of me."

"I know it's my fault," Killian continued. "I acted too fast. But surely there's something you can do!"

Alonzo nodded and went to his desk. From the top drawer he pulled the spear-pole. "Take this," he said, and Killian did. "I want you to kill Rose Geraldine."

"What?" Killian gaped at him. "Why her?"

"Because she talked to that woman from Bones's team. Because she's the one who'll put them on to our plans. And because everyone likes her."

"But what good will her death do?"

"*Think.* If a saurian kills her, it's going to upset everyone. And everyone's going to blame Bones for her death—for stirring up the saurians, for scaring them with his cameras."

A bit stiffly, Killian nodded. "All right, I'll do it. But I think we might be better off lying low."

"Absolutely not," Alonzo said. "Bones is determined to catch us. If the stolen artifacts weren't enough, your shooting the shri certainly will be. And he *will* catch on to us sooner or later; he's a clever man, and clever men are always dangerous. I want him dead—murdered by the miners. When they realize that Bones is responsible for everything that's happened, they're sure to mob him. And that's the only way we're going to be safe."

And, Alonzo thought, *that will also kill Simmons's career.* He smiled.

Killian hefted his spear-pole, wrapped it in paper until it wasn't recognizable, and started for the door. It would soon be dark, the perfect time for the saurians to strike.

Chapter Thirteen

Just after breakfast the next morning, Zeke and his friends left for the beach. The flight took a little over an hour by jumpcar, and as they flew, they chatted about old friends and old times. Zeke found his mood strangely lightening, as though by putting aside his worries for a short time he'd somehow renewed himself.

Finally, the ocean came into sight, a vast expanse of blue-green that was stretched, unbroken, to the horizon. A long sandy beach offered the perfect picnic spot.

Jackson landed the jumpcar twenty meters from the water. Zeke and Sylvie were the first out, and they looked at the sand critically. It was like nothing Zeke had ever seen before.

Mile after mile of yellow-white beach stretched to either side, completely empty of all life. Only strings of some gray-green kelplike plant that had washed up at the tideline showed evidence of life beyond the alien grass behind them.

The water looked more inviting; large combers rolled in off a choppy green ocean. The waves' foam looked green rather than the white Zeke expected—probably due to plankton or something similar, he thought.

As the others chattered idly about food and fish and adventures on other beaches on other worlds, he slipped off his boots and dug his toes into the sand.

Something sharp cut his foot. He yelped and jumped backwards. The big toe of his left foot throbbed as though stung by an insect.

Jackson was at his side a moment later, a stungun that Zeke hadn't known he was carrying in hand. "What is it," he asked, voice low as he scanned the beach.

"I just stepped on something sharp," Zeke said. He felt himself blush. "Nothing too exciting, I'm afraid."

"Oh." Jackson holstered his stungun and squatted next to Zeke. "You okay?"

Zeke pulled his foot around to where he could see, and found a shard of what looked like yellow glass protruding from his toe. He pulled it out, and blood welled from the wound. The shard was jagged and a good two centimeters long. Jackson passed him a white handkerchief and he dabbed at the flow of blood.

"Better get some antiseptic on that," Jackson said, "and wash it to make sure no sand got in the cut."

Zeke nodded as he slipped his shoes back on. "Great way to start a picnic!" he laughed as he limped over to the jumpcar.

"Nobody take off your shoes," Jackson called to the rest of the party. "This sand has glass in it, and there are lots of knifelike bits."

"Glass?" Siona said. "Ugh!"

"This is without a doubt the most unfriendly planet you've dragged us to yet, Zeke," Marty said. "It's a good thing you have us here to watch out for you."

Sylvie dragged out the first aid kit. "A very pleasant place for a picnic," she said. "Take a walk on the beach and chop your feet to bits."

"It's not so bad," Zeke said. "Komako has its advantages."

"Name one!"

"No ants?"

Sylvie snorted and raised a can of plastiflesh. "This is going to sting," she said, "and I'm glad. No ants, indeed!"

Zeke rolled up his pant leg and she sprayed his toe. The stuff burned as it bonded to his skin—but there was nothing better for a cut.

A moment later he had a new layer of artificial skin covering the puncture wound. The pain had already dulled to a distant throb. The plastiflesh would stay on for about a week, letting his body heal naturally, then dry and flake off. Another of BEC's incidental discoveries while pursuing the mysteries of the IO drive.

"Thanks," he said. Standing, he took a magnifying glass from his pocket and carefully scooped up a handful of the sand. "Interesting," he said, examining it. "It's all glass. Most of it seems to have been worn smooth, but there are still quite a few large jagged pieces." He picked out two more like the one that had cut him, then flicked them to the side. "It resembles the glass used in some of the aboriginals' artifacts. I imagine, if we analyzed it, we'd find it was exactly the same."

"Very interesting indeed," Jackson said. He looked up the beach, at the mile after mile of yellow sand. "We shouldn't eat here, then. If any were to blow into the food . . ."

"Too bad," Siona sighed. "I was looking forward to a picnic."

"We can still have it," Sylvie said. "We'll just move inland, away from the ocean, and find a nice hill."

"First good idea you've had all day," Marty said. "Let's get the fishing over with, already. I'm starving!"

"The suits are in the jumpcar," Jackson said. "Give me a hand?"

It turned out Jackson had packed spacesuits from the *Heinrich Schliemann* in the jumpcar's storage compartment. It was a good choice, Zeke reflected: They were lightweight, allowed complete mobility, and had heavy insulation against extremes of cold and heat. Not only that, each suit carried a four-hour supply of air.

He pulled the first one out, noted it was tailored for Marty, and passed it over. The next one was Jackson's— and that was the last one there.

He looked inquiringly at his bodyguard. "Where's mine?"

"I knew you'd want to stay up here," Jackson said. "Let Marty and me handle the fish."

"I didn't come here to watch," Zeke said, a trifle annoyed. He knew Jackson meant well—but he'd never been one to sit on the sidelines and watch others work.

"He's right, for once," Marty said to him.

"Not you too!"

"Really, Zeke. Siona and Sylvie are great, but they don't know how to operate the jumpcar the way you do. And if anything happens to us in the water, I want someone up here who can pull us out. Just like in the Legion, you always leave one of your best men as backup. You should remember that."

"Exactly," Jackson said. He grinned at Marty. "Siona must be having a civilizing effect on you. I think we've agreed on more things here than ever before."

"You're just coming around to my way of thinking," Marty said. He turned his white-in-black eyes on Zeke. "Well?"

Zeke just sighed, knowing the two of them were right, but still not liking it. He had been near the top of his class at the Academy when it came to seat-of-your-pants flying . . . and the safety of his friends had to come before his own feelings.

Finally he nodded. "All right, I'll stay ashore *this* time. I guess I'll just have to entertain the ladies all by myself." He grinned. *Perhaps there are some advantages after all*, he thought.

Jackson paused. "You know, if I didn't know better, I'd think you planned it this way."

Zeke laughed. "You know I'd trade places with you if I could. Suit up." He picked up a bubble helmet while Jackson and Marty began untabbing their shirts. "Let's get this over with as soon as possible—we've still got a picnic to have, remember!"

Entering the ocean was like entering another world, Jackson Charles thought as he waded out chest deep in the water. He glanced at the instrument display on his wrist, checking his suit's readings—just a tad short of four hours of air, with the recycling and heat exchange systems working at maximum efficiency. Next he checked the nets and specimen bags at his belt: all there. Satisfied, he activated his suit's radio.

"Your equipment showing green?" he asked.

"All clear," Zeke said from the jumpcar. "Water temperature reading a delightful fourteen degrees."

"How about you, Marty?"

"I'm fine, of course," Marty said. "I know how to check my suit. Did you want help with yours?"

"No," said Jackson, biting back an angry comment. Marty was like that, and one simply had to live with it. "Ready to go under?"

"A-OK."

"Let's go, then." He turned, waved once to Zeke and the others on shore by the jumpcar, then ducked his head and dove forward.

Water foamed over his helmet, and for an instant he heard the crash of a breaker. Then suddenly he was completely underwater. It was eerily silent, with only the faintest hiss of static from the radio. A green light filtered down from the surface, giving the algae-coated rocks a distinctly unreal look. Here and there small silvery animals darted, fishlike but flat and triangular, their bodies horizontal to the ocean floor. Getting a few of those would be their first task; then they'd move on to larger game.

He glanced to the left, at Marty, who gave him the age-old thumbs-up signal that all was well.

"Let's go," he said, and kicked himself forward and down, following the ocean floor as it curved away and out.

Drawing the small-mesh net from his belt, he began to unfold it so that it trailed out behind him. Marty took the other end and began to circle around, drawing several of the small alien fish into their trap.

Days off from work were always welcome to Dave Szycek. He walked along the rim of the west pit, holding hands with Doreen Green—Mean Green, most of the others called her; he'd been the first to see past her rough-and-tumble exterior to the warm, gentle woman underneath.

They'd been hanging together for the last three months, and they'd already begun to talk about Commitments and Deep Meanings and Truth. Dave had been the one to suggest the walk.

It was a beautiful day, with a warm breeze. Doreen was in a romantic mood (he'd made sure of that!). He planned to ask her to marry him.

He stopped, taking her hand. "Doreen—" he began.

And she screamed in horror.

Dave froze, stomach doing flip-flops. Then he realized she was looking past him, down into the west pit.

He turned—and saw the woman's body on the floor of the pit. She'd evidently fallen; dark lines radiated from her body in a splatter pattern.

"Come on," he said, pulling her away. "Whoever it is, she's dead, and has been that way for a while. We'll report it and let the supervisors take care of it—"

All thoughts of marriage had fled; now wasn't the time. He cursed his luck.

They hurried back toward their camp.

Zeke turned the radio's volume up as high as it would go, then moved away from the jumpcar to join Sylvie and Siona. They'd spread a heavy plastic sheet—heavy enough that the glass couldn't puncture it—over several square meters of sand and now sprawled there watching the waves roll in.

"You just missed them go in," Siona told him. "Marty was so brave, it made my heart skip a beat."

"Uh-huh," Sylvie said, not sounding very convinced.

"There's not much we can do for them except wait," Zeke said. He turned to Sylvie. "How about playing that interview one more time? I'd really like another look."

"I'll get it," Sylvie said. "I put it in my bag before we left." She stood and headed for the jumpcar.

Siona sighed and leaned her chin on her fists, gazing out at the ocean.

Zeke leaned back and closed his eyes. The breeze felt good on his face, warm and friendly, just ruffling his short hair. With the murmur of surf, he might have been back on Earth, he thought, baking on some balmy Mediterranean island. Only the calls of the birds were missing.

Feet crunched on sand. He opened one eye.

"Here you are," Sylvie said, tossing him the holocube.

He caught it and flicked it to play, setting it on his chest. Colors rippled, then once more he gazed at the bar scene, at the miner Rose as she talked to Sylvie.

At the camp cantina, tempers were flaring. Over a hundred miners had packed into the main room. They looked up at the bar, where Julius MacIntyre stood. MacIntyre had been speaking for an hour.

Now he raised the saurian spear-pole that had killed Rose. Dried blood stained its point. He shook the spear-pole with righteous indignation, and a moan of anger came from the miners before him.

"Three dead now!" he called. He looked across the sea of faces and saw the twin fires of anger and fear smoldering there. "Three of our brothers and sisters *killed* by the saurians! Where will it stop? When we're *all* dead, like poor Rose?" His voice broke; he sobbed, "I loved her like a mother. And she's dead now, all because of *Dr. Bones!*"

Murmurs of agreement came from the crowd.

"We all know it's the saurians doing it. Bones and his men have stirred them up by stealing sacred artifacts from their tunnels. The cameras were the last straw! *I* say it isn't worth it! Leave them alone and they'll leave us alone, too!"

The group stirred and let out a collective hiss of frustration Julius MacIntyre looked at his friends, his co-workers. One by one he made contact with each of them. They tended to flinch and look away, uneasy, upset.

"Which one of us is next?" he said. "Your daughter, Harry? Bill Thompson's wife? *You?* Which one of us will they kill because of *Bones?*"

Someone shouted from the back, "What can we do?"

"Destroy their excavation!" a man called from the side.

"Seal up the tunnels!" called another.

"*Now* is the time!" MacIntyre shouted, louder than the rest. He leaped down from the bar and started for the door. *"Do it while there's still daylight!"*

As a group, they surged after him, shouting up their courage, pushing each other on.

They headed for the tool sheds.

When they had gone, Felix Alonzo stirred in the dark booth at the back of the cantina, stretched, and finally stood. The miners would keep Bones and his men more than busy. He smiled. The miners might even *kill* Bones, if luck held—and how would mutiny and riot look on Simmons's record?

Whistling cheerfully, he started after the miners. He'd watch from a safe distance, he decided. It might even be fun, seeing Bones die.

Chapter Fourteen

It was growing dark when they finally started back from the picnic. First stop was the landing field, where Jackson and Zeke loaded one of the robodrones with the alien fish, bits of sand, and samples of grass.

It was a simple matter to program its course and set it for takeoff. After retreating a safe distance, they watched it launch, thrusters flaring, and head into the clouds for the *Ostrum*.

"How soon do you think Cal and Harry will have answers for us?" Sylvie asked.

"Knowing them," Zeke said, "they'll dig in immediately and keep updating us until we're tired of hearing from them."

Only when the robodrone had completely vanished did they head for their camp. On the way, Zeke found himself looking back on the day. He felt curiously satisfied. Despite the stolen artifacts, despite all the problems and puzzles Camelot offered, he felt oddly content.

He knew why: Today was the first day in over a year that he'd forced all his worries aside and allowed himself to relax and actually have fun. Cal and Harry would be starting the first of their tests soon; tomorrow would be time enough to deal with whatever they discovered.

Marty burst in upon his introspection. "Zeke! Take a look below—at the miners' camp!"

That snapped him back to full alertness. He leaned forward and peered out the window.

Perhaps fifty men and women in the gray uniforms of miners had just left their town in a mob—and they were heading for the excavation camp. They carried bright lanterns and what looked like shovels and picks.

"Lynch mob?" Jackson called back.

"Perhaps," Zeke said. "Better get us back fast, so Reelys doesn't have to deal with them alone."

Jackson sent the jumpcar roaring forward, and Zeke's stomach began to knot up. *As if we need more trouble from the miners*, he thought.

He used the jumpcar's communicator to call Simmons. The camp's communications officer put him through at once, and the planetary supervisor answered a moment later from his dinner table.

"What can I do for you tonight, Dr. Bones?"

Zeke didn't bother with niceties. "There are miners heading for my camp with weapons, and they don't look friendly."

"You haven't heard, then," Simmons said. "A miner was found this morning with a spear-pole through her back. I thought I'd gotten everyone calmed down, but something seems to have stirred them up. I'll get my men out there as soon as I can."

"Thanks—" Zeke started, but Simmons had already hung up. *Mustering his forces*, he thought. *He'd just better hurry.*

Jackson was circling down toward the excavation camp by then. The place blazed with light; Reelys had turned on the arc lamps around the buildings, and now nobody could approach without being seen. Two guards stood watching from beside the storage shed from which the artifacts had been stolen. It was locking the bam after the horse had escaped, Zeke knew, but there were still enough artifacts inside that he didn't want to take chances.

He climbed out first, and the others followed on his heels. Reelys floated over leisurely.

"Welcome back, Ezekiel. I trust it was a good trip?"

"There's no time for that now," Zeke said, and he quickly outlined what was happening. "Reelys—you take Siona and Sylvie to the guest house. Don't come back until you hear it's safe from me personally."

"Certainly, Ezekiel," Reelys said. She started toward Siona, speaking softly and quickly.

"I'm staying," Sylvie said. "I don't need to be handed over to—"

"I don't have time to argue," Zeke said. "Go or stay, it's up to you. But keep out of the way so you don't get hurt."

"Will do."

"Marty, keep an eye out for the miners." Zeke went on. "Let me know when they're five minutes away."

"Right, Doc." He grabbed a pair of nightsight binoculars from the worktable and ran up the hill toward the miners' camp, as serious as Zeke had ever seen him.

Then Zeke called the two guards over and explained the situation to them. The two men glanced at each other, then nodded that they understood. "We'll keep them back, sir," said one. Unshouldering their energy rifles, they took up positions at the edge of camp.

Meantime, Jackson had gone into the middle storage shed—which held their lockers of equipment—and had unsealed the case containing weapons. He flipped back its lid, revealing a row of sleek black stunguns, the latest and most efficient models. They were a standard part of every excavation now. Zeke Bones had met too much trouble on too many alien worlds to go out unprepared. He hated to resort to violence, but there were too many people in the galaxy who only understood force.

Jackson started clicking powerpacks into the stunguns' butts and handing them out. Zeke tucked two into his belt, and took two more for Marty.

Marty returned a few seconds later, panting. "They're heading this way, all right," he said, "carrying weapons and moving fast. Five minutes before they get here, Doc."

Zeke gave Marty his two stunguns. "As I told the guards," he said, "the object's not going to be to drive them off. It's going to be to hold them back until Simmons can get more of his men out here. It's just the five of us until then."

"We've been outnumbered before," Marty said, grinning happily. "It'll be like the good old days."

Zeke took another pair of stunguns and turned to Sylvie. "I really wish you'd go with Reelys," he said. "I don't know what's going to happen, but these are rough frontier people, and there's no telling what they'll do. At least protect yourself and take a stungun."

She shook her head. "It violates my ethics as a journalist. Those who don't carry guns generally don't get shot."

"We must go now," Reelys said. "Are you sure you want to stay, Sylvie?"

"I said so, didn't I? I've been through bigger fights than this before. Now hurry up and get Siona out of here."

"I want to stay with you," Siona said to Marty, who struck a valiant pose with his stungun.

"I won't hear of it," he said. "You go with Reelys. If you were here, I'd only worry about your safety."

Siona sighed dreamily. "Now I know why I love you!" She gave him a quick peck on the cheek, then followed Reelys out of the circle of light, into darkness and safety.

Jackson pulled the rack of stunguns out of the locker. Underneath, nestled in little cushioned pockets, lay twelve handsized silver spheres with pull tabs—percussion grenades.

Zeke's eyes widened in surprise. "What are you doing with those? I thought I said no weapons beyond stunguns!"

"I know you did," Jackson said, pulling out four and stuffing them into his pockets. "But my job's to protect you, and I decided to bring them anyway. If we needed them, they'd be here. If we didn't need them, you wouldn't have known." He slammed down the weapons locker's lid and started for the door. "Set your stungun's charge to maximum," he said. "I think the grenades and a few well-placed threats will be enough to turn them back . . . but be ready for anything."

He ran outside and ducked around behind one of the storage sheds, out of sight. Zeke knew he was taking up a position to throw the grenades.

They could hear the rumble of the miners' voices now, loud and angry as they approached. Then the mob topped the next hill over like a swarm of ants. Seeing Bones and his camp, they let out a howl of rage and indignation.

In a mass, they stormed forward. Simmons's two guards took steps back, hesitant, but raised their rifles and prepared to fire.

"Don't shoot," Zeke said, behind them. "Wait for—"

The rest of his words vanished in a deafening *crack* of sound, like a thunderbolt but louder still, and so long it seemed to stretch across minutes rather than seconds.

Jackson had thrown the first of his percussion grenades.

Zeke covered his ears. Marty and Sylvie did the same. Still the sound rolled on.

Then two more *cracks* of sound followed, and the miners began dropping their weapons and lights and screaming in pain. They were at the center of the grenades' explosions and felt the effects most sharply.

Zeke stepped forward. "Go back to your camp!" he shouted as loudly as he could. "You will only be hurt if you continue here!"

The three men nearest him uncovered their ears and started forward, glaring their hatred. Marty fired with all the calmness and precision that only years in the Legion of Ares could give. The three crumpled and fell, unconscious.

The rest of the miners fell back more slowly, with dark mutterings and angry looks. Finally they turned and slunk away into the darkness.

Only then did Zeke hear the thrum of approaching jumpcars. The cavalry was arriving—too late to do any good.

Jackson rejoined them. "They won't be back," he said confidently. "At least, not tonight."

"We're going to have to do something about them," Marty said. "Ship 'em off to their new pit and make 'em stay there—*something.*"

"I'll let Simmons take care of it," Zeke said. "They're his men, and he's responsible for them. He'll know what to do." He sat down. Suddenly his guts did flip-flops, and he felt violently ill. He cradled his head in his hands, pressed his eyes shut, and took a series of deep, calming breaths. He felt a million years old, the weight of centuries pressing down on him.

When he next looked up, some minutes later, he found Jackson watching him with concern.

"Are you all right?" he asked.

Zeke nodded. "Tension, I think."

"You're pale as bone."

"My stomach hurts."

He shook his had. "Maybe Reelys should take a look at you tomorrow."

"I think so."

"Go lie down. Simmons's men can keep watch. I don't think the miners will dare come back tonight. Maybe tomorrow, when they've worked themselves up to it, but not tonight."

"They won't be back." Zeke said it with conviction. "Simmons will see to that." He took the arm Jackson offered and pulled himself to his feet. "And I think you're right," he continued, and started for the hut where the artifacts were kept. "I'd better take a rest, while I still can."

There was a cot inside; it would be just like his days in the Academy of Mars.

"See you tomorrow," Jackson said.

Zeke smiled thinly. "You can bet on it."

When Dr. Bones stormed in to see him the next morning, the last Knight wasn't surprised. In fact, he'd been expecting it. He greeted Bones calmly, then cut to the heart of the matter.

"I can only offer my apologies. It was a regrettable incident, but I've taken measures to see that nothing like it happens again. There's not much more I can do."

"How did it start, exactly?"

"Julius MacIntyre—one of our demolitions people—seems to have been the ringleader. He stirred everyone up with a speech in the cantina, then led them to your camp to destroy it so—as he says—'the saurians will leave us alone.' That's all I've been able to get out of anyone."

"What happened to him?"

"He's in a detention cell. He'll be shipped out on the next freighter, as soon as I'm convinced he doesn't know anything more."

"You don't have reason to suspect him of anything else, do you?"

Simmons shook his head. "No. He was a good man, and I'll be sorry to lose him. It's routine to hold him and question him for two weeks. Otherwise I'd just ship him out on the *Constellation* and be done with it,"

Bones looked surprised. "The *Constellation's* still here?"

"More drive trouble, but it should be fixed by tomorrow."

"Good. Now, what about those artifacts? And tell me more about the miner who was killed."

The last Knight proceeded to tell him all he knew—which, he hated to admit, wasn't all that much.

Killian paced angrily, and Felix Alonzo watched him in a moody silence. Nothing had gone according to plan.

Who would have thought they'd have grenades and stun-guns? Alonzo wondered. *They're supposed to be archaeologists, not soldiers.* Vaguely he remembered—too late now—something in a vid about Bones having served in the Legion of Ares.

"We've got to do something about MacIntyre!" Killian said at last. "Kill him!"

"Don't be bloodthirsty. You should never kill without reason. What good would it do—except to make everyone more suspicious than ever?"

"He's addicted to narcodrine. If they find out, they'll want to know where he's getting it. And if he tells them, they'll know about us."

"Correction," Alonzo said. "They'll know about *you*."

"What's that supposed to mean?" Killian demanded. "We're in this together. As partners."

"Correction," Alonzo said. "We *were*." And he drew a stungun from under the table and fired it point-blank at Killian's head.

Killian crumpled to the floor, unconscious, breathing heavily. Standing, Alonzo kicked him once in the side. Ribs cracked.

"Fool," he muttered. "At least you can be of service one last time." And he went to get one final alien artifact, an axe he'd found and saved for his own personal use many months before.

Later still that afternoon, the last Knight Inquisitor sat at his round table, reading the reports his man-at-arms had just brought in. The pictures were . . . grisly.

The first showed a man—Killian—with most of his head chopped off by a saurian axe. The blade of that axe was still imbedded in his skull.

The second showed a woman he didn't recognize lying face-down in a pool of blood, a saurian spear-pole protruding from her back. He checked the report. Fritta Korowalski was her name. He remembered her now—Granny, everyone called her; she had been well-liked and her death brought a lump to his throat.

They'd both been found in the hills near Bones's camp. More saurian work, Alonzo had said. And it was almost enough to convince him there really *were* saurians still about, despite the planetary survey, despite the assurances of Bones and his people. What miner could have been so unfeeling, so callous, as to kill Granny? Or so ruthless, so bloodthirsty, to have killed Killian in such a manner? He shuddered at the thought.

And as if those two deaths weren't enough, the report noted damage to the drive mechanisms of three more rock-crushers. They could be repaired in time, but it was a good three- or four-day overhaul. And his techs were already running low on spare parts—Wagner hadn't brought more than the standard replacements. Which meant they'd fall even further behind schedule.

He poured himself a large brandy, drained it, then stood. *Time to see MacIntyre*, he thought. The detention cells were in the next building; normally they were used for miners who'd had too much to drink and needed time to dry out—or time to cool off after a brawl.

The walk over cleared his mind a little. He was almost sober, in fact, when he went into the detention building.

"Sir!" said the man on duty by the door, standing behind his desk. "About MacIntyre—I think something's wrong with him. I was just making out a report on it—"

Simmons waved him to silence. "Start from the beginning," he said. "What's wrong?"

"Yes, sir. He used to just lie in his bunk, but for the last hour he's been pacing and pounding on the walls. And he's been screaming something about his skin burning—"

"That sounds familiar," Simmons said, puzzled, trying to remember where he'd heard about burning skin before.

"It's a common withdrawal symptom from narcodrine, sir." "Narcodrine? Where would he get *that*?" "Perhaps . . ." The man bit his lip. "There are always ways, sir. On every mining planet."

"I suppose," Simmons said slowly, shocked. "Have him tested. I don't want to talk to him when he's in a state like that. And I don't want anyone else finding out about his symptoms until he's been verified. Understand?"

"Yes, sir."

Simmons turned and stalked back to his office, more bewildered than ever. *Narcodrine.* He shuddered at the very name. It produced a remarkable high—but tended to burn out the central nervous system over the years. And if one of his people had it, how many more did?

A call came for Zeke from the *Ostrum* that afternoon. He took it at once.

It was Cal. "Those fish you sent up," he said, "are rather odd. They all carry a sort of genetic parasite, which their RNA has partially neutralized."

"Genetic parasite?" Zeke said. "I'm not sure I quite follow you."

"It's rather simple, Doc. Think of it this way: Any creature's genetic structure contains nooks and crannies where things can be hidden. Certain viruses and diseases are carried that way. But the strange part is that this genetic parasite seems to be an artificial construct. It does *something,* and I think it has to do with nitrogen, but I'm not sure quite what. Its makeup also seems to resemble the spores of the grass you sent up. There may be a correlation, and we're checking on it now."

"Is this parasite going to pose any danger to humans?"

"I doubt a human could catch it. And if someone managed to, it wouldn't have any effect. We're pretty weird biologically, compared to this planet's native stock. But I'd be willing to bet the thing spread like wildfire through all the native animals when it was first introduced."

"Perhaps that's why there aren't any land creatures left."

"It might well be. We've isolated it now, and we're running tests. We should have a definitive report by tomorrow."

"Thanks," Zeke said. "That's more than I'd hoped for."

Alonzo felt the net closing in around him, and he didn't like the feeling. The murders of Granny and Killian should have created quite a stir, brought the miners back to the boiling point, but instead they seemed to have had the opposite effect. Now people were sticking close to their camp, only traveling in groups, and taking extra cautions to avoid any mention of the saurians or their tunnels.

And, worse, MacIntyre had started to show signs of narcodrine withdrawal. He'd seen the report through his job with security. They'd already tested MacIntyre for it. And Simmons had begun asking people about the drug, whether anyone had a supply; of course, he'd discovered nothing—but the fact that he was asking questions was a bad sign. Fortunately MacIntyre's test results weren't back yet, but it would only be a matter of hours now.

Alonzo needed something really large, really messy, to distract everyone. He needed something which would occupy Bones and Simmons.

He needed to cover his ass before things got worse.

What do you do when too many people know too much? he wondered. *Can I possibly kill them all?*

Chapter Fifteen

The next call from the *Ostrum* came early the following morning, well before Zeke had expected it. He got up from breakfast and went into the guest house study to take it alone.

When he flicked on the monitor, he found a very tired-looking Cal on the other end. He didn't think his friend had slept at all that night.

"Any news?" Zeke said.

Cal nodded. "The parasite's a complicated mess, but things are finally starting to make sense. It's similar in structure to some old terrestrial germ-warfare viruses. It reacts with nitrogen to form a deadly poison in the bloodstream. Interestingly, the virus is present in all of the sea animals; they seem to have somehow become immune to it."

"It's definitely an artificial construct, though, not something that evolved here?"

"We're certain. It's too virulent a mutation to occur naturally. There are checks and balances that would have killed it."

"But how does it work?"

"Ah, now that's where the interesting part comes in. There's a very complex life cycle for the parasite. It's produced in the grass's seed-pods. When the plants' spoors are inhaled or ingested, they split into smaller parts, some of which attach themselves to RNA strands and begin modifying genetic codes."

"A plant attacking an animal," Zeke said.

"And on the microscopic level. That's doubtless how land animals became extinct on this planet. I'm working from pure conjecture at this point, but I'd be willing to bet there's another, milder variety of the grass which grows wild in the ocean. The land grass was doubtless adapted from it. The marine life had been ingesting the mild kind, and so had a partial immunity to the poison when the deadly variety was introduced to the ecosystem. That's why there's still ocean life here, rather than a vast soup of plankton."

"So you don't think there could be any land animals alive anywhere on Komako?"

"Not unless they've been protected in some way against the spoors. Judging from the parasite and the planetary survey, I'd say it's a virtual impossibility."

"Thanks," Zeke said. "That's what I needed to know."

"We'll keep working and see what else we can come up with," Cal said, "but I'm afraid it's just going to be technical refinements from here."

"You've already given me more than I expected. Why don't you take a break? You look ready to drop."

Cal grinned. "You get the same way whenever you're in the middle of an exciting discovery."

"So do as I say, not as I do!"

"Sure, Doc." He didn't look like he planned to take that advice. "Talk to you soon."

"Bye."

When the screen went dark, Zeke sat back and thought about Cal's information for a time. A new puzzle had presented itself.

The grass had been artificially produced, but the artifacts they'd found in the tunnels didn't indicate a culture advanced enough for genetic engineering. *But that's what archaeologists fifty thousand years from now would think if they excavated a few places on Earth,* he thought. Perhaps this had been a backwater settlement and, halfway across the continent, there had been some central point of high civilization. It was a large planet; he didn't doubt the possibility.

Finally he went back to breakfast. As soon as he stepped into the room, everyone stopped eating and looked at him expectantly.

"I've got good news and bad news," he said, and he proceeded to tell of Cal's and Harry's discoveries. They all sat in startled silence until he'd finished.

It was Jackson who spoke first. "But the saurians were clearly sentient," he said. "Wouldn't they have found a way to destroy the spoors? And why create the grass at all?"

Zeke shrugged. "Who knows? Perhaps they had a cultural or religious taboo against killing living things, even grass. Or perhaps they were involved in some war or genetic experiment and it just got out of hand. We'll probably never know, since they don't seem to have left any written or pictorial records."

"That still does not solve our immediate problem," Reelys whistled. "We need to discover who is sabotaging the equipment, and who is behind the theft of the artifacts."

"You know," Sylvie said, "perhaps you've been pursuing this from the wrong angle. We've been assuming that it's been the miners sabotaging the equipment—but when you think about it, they might not be the best suspects. After all, they're better off here than on any other mining planet I've ever seen. Why would they want to stir things up and create problems for themselves?"

"Greed?" Marty suggested. "Humans are always pushing for more and better—"

Zeke shook his head. "I think you're right," he told Sylvie. "There must be something else at the root of the trouble. But what?"

"Perhaps you were too quick to dismiss my first thought, Ezekiel," Reelys said.

"The black market?"

"Yes."

Zeke frowned. He thought again of his father's private collection, how many alien worlds had been plundered just for the amusement of one rich man. He didn't want to face the possibility of black marketeers operating on Camelot—but were there any other options?

He'd start from the beginning and work his way forward logically. That seemed the best solution.

He said, "If we eliminate the saurians and the miners as suspects, that only leaves the supervisors and their support personnel. And Simmons knew nothing about the theft—I *know* that. Everyone else has been psychoscreened for service here."

"There are ways around psychoscreening," Siona said suddenly. "It's just a conditioning method to insure loyalty to the company. If a person were serving both the company and himself, or was convinced he was serving both, then that might well allow him to become a thief or smuggler on the side."

Marty looked at her in surprise. "How did you know all that?"

She smiled demurely. "I was psychoscreened for a job I once had."

Zeke said, "Perhaps it's time I had another talk with Simmons. Jackson? Why don't you come with me."

"And me," Marty said quickly.

"*No!*" Zeke and Jackson said as one.

The last Knight ushered the King into his office. It was an expected visit. The King had called him up and asked to see him. Of course, the last Knight could not refuse.

He sat back and listened while the King told him of the genetic parasite in the fish, how its life cycle began with the alien grass. He began to grow alarmed as the story unfolded, but the King assured him humans would be immune.

"So where does that leave us?" he asked.

The King leaned forward. "Someone here—some *human*—is responsible for sabotaging your equipment, murdering your miners, and stealing my artifacts. If we eliminate you and all the miners, who's left?"

"Just a few people," he said slowly. "But they're all psychoscreened—"

"Let's assume they're no longer psychoscreened," the King said. "Let's assume they found a way around it, or the process failed in some way. Who would that leave?"

"The supervisors . . . Felix Alonzo, Joe Clay, Armond Herlekov, Jon Piege, and Killian—but he's dead."

"Dead?" the King's assistant asked, eyes narrowing. "How?"

"Two more murders." He dug the pictures from a folder and passed them over.

Bones studied them in silence for a moment, then passed them to Jackson. "Who else is left?" he asked.

"Our office workers, the communications officers, pay-master, minister, two teachers . . . perhaps thirty more. If I had to suspect someone, I wouldn't know where to begin."

Slowly the King nodded. "I've discussed it with my people, and we'd like to explore the possibilities of the theft being tied in with black marketeers. Are you aware of any black market activity on Komako?"

Simmons just sat there for a startled second. *Does he know about MacIntyre?* he wondered.

Finally he said, "I wasn't aware of any until yesterday. The miner who led the attack on your camp turned out to be a narcodrine addict. But I haven't been able to find out where he's been getting the stuff."

"Narcodrine is nasty," Jackson said, "and it's also expensive, as I remember. You'd need a well-equipped laboratory to make it. It couldn't have come from Komako."

"I agree," the last Knight said. "It won't be much longer before he tells us where he got it. Withdrawal symptoms are rather painful, and he's been told he won't receive anything to ease the pain until he talks."

The King nodded slowly. "When he does, let me know. But that still leaves the problem of how the drugs and artifacts are getting to and from the planet. Do you have a starship schedule? How many ships call here regularly?"

"I don't have to look it up to tell you. Yours is the first unscheduled visit we've had in nearly two years. Only the ore freighters stop by—one every three months, like clockwork."

"Then that must be how the drugs arrive—and how the artifacts are going to be smuggled off-world . . . if they haven't already left with Wagner."

Simmons paused. "The *Constellation* is still in orbit with drive problems, as I told you . . ."

"Ah . . ." The King thought long and hard. "Can you keep her there? I want my men to take a look at her cargo holds."

"Wagner won't cooperate."

"I don't care whether he cooperates or not. I'm going to have his ship searched. I *can* get written authority to back up my actions, if I have to."

"That's not what I meant," Simmons said quickly. "I'm not sure he'd listen if I ordered him to let you search his ship. My authority, technically, only extends to this planet and its people. I'm sure he'd resent it if I started ordering him about. Freighter pilots are . . . *difficult*, if you know what I mean. You've met him. You know what long periods alone in space can do to a man. I have no idea how he'd react."

Bones frowned. "I believe you mentioned him being the only one aboard his ship?"

"That's right."

"Then get him down here. Make up a reason, if you have to. As soon as he's off his ship, let me know—I'll have the technicians on the *Ostrum* fly over and have a look. If there's nothing unusual, no harm done. But if the stolen artifacts *are* there, then I'll bet Wagner will lead us to the rest of the people involved."

"Very well," Simmons said. "But I hope—I *pray*—you're wrong about this. If you are and Wagner finds out, he won't take it lightly."

"But he'd also be cleared of all suspicion," the King said, "which might be just as important.

It was Felix Alonzo's turn to pace. Between the problems with Bones and the problems with MacIntyre and

Killian, he wasn't in a mood for patience. He couldn't get rid of the feeling that all his plans were slowly unraveling around him. Until Wagner left with the artifacts, he wouldn't feel safe—and he wasn't sure he'd feel safe even then.

"What's to be done?" Clay asked.

Felix Alonzo paused for only a second. He'd been wondering that himself for the last few hours. What *did* you do when the authorities were closing in? What last resources did you call upon?

Then it came to him: *money.* Between the black market and his own private accounts, he could lay his hands on quite a bit of cash. Every man had his price—even Dr. Ezekiel Bones.

"We'll buy him off," he said. "You'll have to go speak to him, make him an offer he can't refuse."

"Me?" Clay said. "Why not you?"

"Because," Alonzo said, "I give the orders, and I think it's safest for you to go." *And if necessary, I can kill you to protect myself.*

"I don't like it."

"You don't have to. You just have to do it."

"Right," Clay said reluctantly. "I'll go tonight, when it's dark."

The communicator beeped, and Zeke flicked the vidiscreen back.

"Wagner is on his way down," Simmons said. "I told him we're having some trouble with the recalibration, and it's going to take a couple of days to straighten out, so he might as well come down here until then. He agreed."

"Thanks," Zeke said. "I'll tell my men."

He severed the connection, then called Cal and Harry aboard the *Ostrum* and gave them their instructions.

"Take a look at this," Marty called to Zeke. "I think I've got a picture of your saurians!"

Zeke set down his catalog of artifacts and came to stand behind Marty. "How'd you come up with it?"

The computer monitor showed a series of grid lines that bisected a three-dimensional figure. Marty adjusted the controls and the grid disappeared and the creature's body solidified, becoming a buglike creature with short legs and arms, colored in various shades of browns. Plates halfway between an exoskeleton and skin covered its body.

Its hands seemed most familiar, but had six thick, stubby fingers, two of which were opposable thumbs. All limbs and digits had too many joints.

The face looked completely alien. The thing had four eye-stalks on top of its head, a series of slits that looked more like gills than a nose, and a puckered round mouth. It had no ears or hair. In fact, it resembled a xenobiologist's nightmare, Zeke thought.

Marty just grinned proudly, like a child showing off a new toy. "I realized the cilia on the fish we caught came in sixes, just like the fingers on the creatures. It wasn't hard to extrapolate a larger, land-adapted version."

"Mmm . . . what did Reelys say about it?"

"S/he thought it was a good idea. Zeke, the thing's a monster, but I know I'm close. So what if the skin's a bit off, or the color's wrong, or the brain cavity isn't big enough? That's our alien. It could walk, it could use tools, and it could *think*. What more could you want?"

"An internal skeleton."

"Picky, picky. Oh—and take a look at its back." He rotated the figure on the screen.

Zeke leaned forward. The creature had two series of hard plates, one to the left and one to the right, running the length of its body. The spine—if spine it was—had been left unprotected, probably for greater mobility, just like in the fish they'd caught.

"Am I supposed to see something?"

"Think about the statues," Marty said. "I kept looking at them and saying to myself, 'Why would a race of practical creatures make statues when the only other artifacts they left were tools?' And then I looked at their backs and suddenly it all made sense."

"Chairs," Zeke said suddenly.

"That's right." Marty smiled with incredible smugness. "Simple, huh?"

Zeke nodded slowly. "I suppose the statues don't look all that dragonlike when you think about it. They only looked that way when you were told they were dragons. The power of suggestion."

"Simmons named the planet Camelot," Marty said. "I guess he has dragons on his mind."

Zeke laughed. "That's quite a discovery. Have you told anyone else?"

"Not yet."

"I'll send Siona and Sylvie over—they're watching the tunnels on the monitors. That way you can impress them, too."

Joe Clay had never liked intrigue. It was a game better suited to people like Killian and Alonzo. He liked the straightforward approach: You do something, you get paid for it, end of subject. His greatest contribution to the smuggling operation had been his bookkeeping and accounting skills.

But with Alonzo scared and Killian dead (by Alonzo's hand—he was sure of that), that left him to do the dirty work. He didn't like it, not at all.

But, in the end, he followed orders. He'd always been a great believer in orders. So he started for Bones's camp at dusk, and arrived just as the excavation's arc lights came on.

The whole group sat together at the main table, talking quietly, looking at something on a computer screen. Two guards patrolled near the sheds where Bones kept his equipment and artifacts.

Clay stopped, felt himself beginning to sweat, and for an instant almost turned back. Then he swallowed, put on a stiff smile, and walked into the light.

The guards waved to him; he waved back, hardly see-ing them. Bones had stood at his presence, and now that he'd committed himself, he couldn't back out.

"Dr. Bones," he said, his voice a squeak, "may I talk to you a minute? In private?"

"Certainly, Joe," Bones said. He crossed over to where Clay stood, and together they strolled to the edge of the camp. "Is this private enough for you?"

"Yes." He swallowed. "I've been sent to, uh, ask you something . . ."

"What?"

"How much do you want?"

Bones shook his head, puzzled. "I don't understand."

"To go away. To forget about Camelot and the exca-vation here. How much money. Just name your price."

"Ah!" Bones said. "I see now. You were sent to do your boss's dirty work."

Nervous, Clay nodded.

"Well, you can go back and tell him or her that I don't deal with middlemen. He or she can come back and we'll discuss it then."

"All right," Clay said. "But no tricks—or you'll regret it."

"Of course," Bones said soothingly. "I know what's in my best interest. I'm sure we'll be able to work something out."

Clay nodded again, curtly, then turned and walked off into the darkness, toward the miners' camp, just like Alonzo had told him to do. He didn't look back.

Zeke strolled back to the table slowly and easily. If someone were watching him from the darkness, he didn't want to give anything away.

Clay had seemed the least likely of Simmons's supervisors to be involved in smuggling. *Or perhaps he was threatened into making the offer for someone else*, Zeke thought. He certainly hadn't been well practiced at bribery.

Sylvie looked at him curiously. "What was that all about?" she asked.

"I got an offer I'm not supposed to refuse," Zeke said. "I can name my own price if I just pick up and leave."

Marty stood, fists clenching. "So Clay's the one! Let's go get him, Zeke!"

"Not so fast," Zeke said, pushing him back into his seat. "Jackson, send one of your servos to follow him. I want to know if he meets anyone. He's not the leader, he's just following orders. I want to know who's responsible before I go chasing people down."

"Oh," Marty said.

Jackson had taken a small gray cube from his pocket and activated it. It sprouted little wings and came to life when he ran a finger down its back. He let it go in the direction Clay had taken, then sat back and closed his eyes. Zeke knew he was following the servo's flight through its remote camera, which relayed its picture to his artificial eye.

"He's entering the miners' camp," Jackson said a few minutes later. "He's alone. He's looking around, like he's afraid he's being watched. Now he's started for the can-tina." Suddenly he gave a startled yelp and jerked back in his chair. His eyes flew open.

"What happened?" Zeke said.

Jackson shook his head grimly. "They were watching for us. Something or someone destroyed the servo."

"They followed you," Alonzo said, nudging the smoldering bit of metal and plastic with the toe of his boot. He'd shot it as it followed Clay down the street. "I thought I told you to be careful."

"I didn't see it," Clay said. "And he said he wanted to cooperate—"

"He was just stringing you along. He wanted to find out who I was, then make his move." He glared into the darkness toward the excavation. "Tell me what he said."

Clay did, in great detail.

When he'd finished, Alonzo just grunted. "I don't like that. It means he's too confident. It means he doesn't want to deal. He must have begun to figure out what's going on. That means we need him stopped *now*."

"What do you want to do?"

"Kill him," Alonzo said. He pressed his energy pistol into Clay's hands. "It's our last hope."

"But—" Clay started.

"*Do it!*" Alonzo said. "That's an order. You don't want to end up like Killian, do you?"

Terrified, Clay just shook his head.

Alonzo faced him toward the excavation and gave him a shove in the small of the back. He stumbled forward. Then he stopped, swallowed, and began the long walk back. The energy pistol felt heavy as lead in his hand, but he didn't dare disobey Felix Alonzo.

The servo's destruction had made him nervous, Zeke knew. Every few minutes he glanced up, expecting to see Clay returning, hopefully with his boss in tow.

Then he caught a glimpse of something pale moving in the darkness. He watched from the corner of his eye, but the person didn't come closer. That made him distinctly uneasy. Then something metallic glinted in the darkness. Gun? Knife?

That decided Zeke. He moved around the side of the table, pretending to look at the computer monitor over Marty's shoulder, putting Jackson between himself and the man.

"We have company," Zeke whispered to his bodyguard, without looking up. "Don't turn around. I think it's Clay again—he's standing just outside the circle of light, looking at us."

"Probably trying to get up his nerve," Jackson said.

"Are you still carrying that stungun?"

"Yes."

"Give it to me. I think he's armed."

Still pretending to look at the computer monitor, Jackson slipped one hand into his jacket and eased the stungun out of its shoulder holster. He was careful to keep his back to Clay, blocking the man's view of Zeke.

Zeke took the stungun without looking at it. "On the count of three," he whispered.

"Right."

"One . . . two . . . *three!*"

And as Jackson leaped to the side, Zeke dropped into position and fired a sweeping shot into the darkness. The dim form he'd taken for Clay crumpled to the ground.

The others at the table were up and staring at him in surprise. The two guards rushed over, looking bewildered.

He grinned at them all. "Still the best shot in the galaxy," he said, and blew across the stungun's barrel.

"Save the theatrics," Marty growled. "You could warn a fellow when you're going to jump like that!"

Jackson climbed to his feet and jogged over to the body. A second later he was back, carrying an unconscious Clay slung over one shoulder. He threw the man to the ground with little ceremony.

"He had an energy pistol," he said. "Probably meant to kill you, Zeke."

"Do you want us to hold him here?" one of the guards asked. "Or should we take him back to a detention cell?"

"Take him to a cell," Zeke said. "Call Simmons and have him meet us there."

Clay had recovered consciousness by the time they reached the detention building. Zeke tried to talk to him, but he only sat there sullenly, staring out the window.

"Look," Marty said, "either you talk or I'm gonna start breaking your fingers. We don't have time for games."

Clay said, "It's against the Statutes to torture prisoners. The most you can do is lock me up pending the planetary supervisor's judgment on the case. I didn't *do* anything!"

"You did enough to get you blacklisted and dumped on an open planet," Zeke said. "But if you were to cooperate, I might see fit to intercede on your behalf. You might even be able to keep your pension."

The jumpcar settled to land. Jackson popped the door.

"If I were to . . . *cooperate*," Clay said, "how do I know you'd help me?"

"I give you my word."

Clay shook his head.

"Isn't that better than ending up like Killian?" Zeke said suddenly, remembering the other murdered supervisor.

When Clay still didn't answer, Jackson seized his arm and pulled him out. The two guards took him from there.

Simmons had been waiting. He shook his head sadly as he watched Clay being led off.

"I never would have suspected him," he said. "I thought he was the most loyal man here. Never late with his reports, never under his sector's quota—"

"The best criminal," Zeke said, "is the one you never suspect."

"I wouldn't doubt it," Simmons said. He sighed. "I do have one bit of news. It seems the man supplying narco-drine was another one of my supervisors, Killian."

"But he's dead!" Jackson said.

"That's right," Simmons said. "So I'm afraid it's no help."

"But perhaps it is," Zeke said suddenly. "It's all starting to fit together piece by piece. My men are searching the *Constellation* now. It's a big freighter, and it's going to take a while, but if anything's there they'll find it. For simplicity's sake, let's assume Wagner is guilty—he's been smuggling drugs down to the planet. And let's assume he's also taken the stolen artifacts aboard, for delivery to the black market that deals in such things."

"Fair enough," Simmons said. "But let's keep in mind that these are only assumptions."

"So we have a tight little group consisting of Wagner, Killian, and Joe Clay. There has to be at least one more person, since Clay's certainly not a killer, and I don't believe he has the brains or stomach to have faked the saurian attacks. Wagner couldn't have done them because he was with us or in orbit when they happened."

"Who would this other person be?" Simmons said.

"Another one of your supervisors. He's got to be the smartest one of the bunch, the one behind all the others, telling them what to do, planning their every move. He'd be smart enough to stay out of trouble at all costs—to do his job supremely well. Mr. Simmons, who *is* your most efficient supervisor?"

"Felix Alonzo," Simmons said without hesitation. "He's smart, and he's devious. I can believe he'd run a smuggling ring!"

"It's easy enough to prove," Zeke said. "Give Clay an hour to brood, then let me talk to him."

Simmons gestured toward the detention building. "Certainly. We can wait in the lounge. After you."

Chapter Sixteen

The detention cells were minimally furnished; they had a cot, a sink, a toilet, and not much else. Only the door had a window, and it was barred.

Zeke looked into Clay's cell and found Clay sitting on the bed, face hidden in his hands.

"Joe," he called.

Clay looked up. His eyes were bloodshot. "What?"

"You don't have to worry about it anymore. Wagner's just been arrested, and he's talking about how you and Felix Alonzo planned the whole drug-smuggling operation."

"That bastard!" Clay screamed. He was on his feet and at the door in a second. "It wasn't me, it was Alonzo! I just kept the records for him!"

Zeke stepped back, smiling. "Thanks," he said. "That's all we wanted to know."

"Hey—" Clay said, a startled look on his face. The enormity of what he'd just said had begun to settle in. "I didn't mean that—"

Simmons was nodding unhappily. He followed Zeke to the door and out to where Marty and Jackson waited with the jumpcar. "I guess you were right, then," he said. "It is Wagner. And Alonzo. I never would have suspected them. Wagner's at my house; I'll have him arrested. And I'll send men to get Alonzo."

"Good idea," Zeke said.

The communicator at his belt beeped. He answered almost absently.

It was Harry. "I'm aboard the *Constellation*," he said. "There are crates of everything from narcodrine to beta pollidox in Wagner's quarters, and Cal says there are more vacuum-packed crates in the holds than show up on the cargo manifests. He didn't open them because he didn't know whether the contents would be hurt by space. Do you want us to open one anyway? We could bring one back to the *Ostrum*."

"That's okay," Zeke said. "I know what's in them."

"That just leaves the drugs. What do you want done with them?"

"Dump them out the airlock."

Harry grinned. "Yes, sir. Anything else?"

"That should about do it."

Felix Alonzo had followed Clay back to Bones's camp an hour earlier. He had watched with frustration as Clay circled just beyond the arc lights' reach, hesitating, unable to bring himself to kill.

And suddenly Bones had dropped into a shooting position and fired a stungun. Clay fell without a sound.

At another time, Alonzo might have stayed and tried the shot himself—he had another energy pistol with him, after all—but somehow he had a bad feeling about it. *I never should have sent Clay*, he thought. *I should have let Killian do it, and then killed him.*

Instead of trying to work things out, he'd panicked. *Run*, an inner voice said. He'd turned and fled back to his house.

He'd packed the few possessions he wanted quickly and efficiently, and as he did, almost absently he'd flipped his communicator to the open channel and left it on.

And so he'd heard Simmons order Wagner and him arrested. Cursing, he'd grabbed his bags and headed for the jumpcars. He'd have to get to Wagner first, he knew. The two of them could steal a shuttle and get to the *Constellation*, and from there it would be an easy enough escape. He had friends in high places who could cover for him. And the artifacts in the *Constellation*'s holds would give them all the money they needed.

The excavation camp buzzed with activity. Sylvie had taken Reelys and recovered her holocams, and now wandered among the party, filming "the spectacular end to one of the most daring crime rings the universe has ever seen," as she called it. Marty was only too happy to be the first one interviewed, giving a story that portrayed him as quite a bit more heroic than he actually had been. Siona formed a rapt audience.

Zeke just sighed. *As if I need more stories about me on the vids*, he thought.

"'Ezekiel," Reelys said, floating over to him. "Are you sure you want to be out here like this? I would feel much safer if you were to spend the rest of the night inside the guest house."

"Nonsense," he said. "You saw Simmons put twenty guards around the camp in case Alonzo tries anything. What could happen now?"

Jackson joined them. "I just heard the news from one of the guards," he said. "They just brought Wagner to the detention cells. That only leaves Alonzo free."

"And any other men he might have," Reelys said.

Zeke laughed. "You worry too much. There's no place for Alonzo to go. He's a smart man—"

"A *desperate* man," Reelys whistled.

"—and he'll see there's no hope in his situation. I wouldn't be surprised if he gave himself up."

Six paces by eight paces, Wagner thought, glowering at his cell's walls. *I want out now.* What he'd do to Simmons when he found him wouldn't be pretty.

As if three months at a time in the *Constellation*'s crew quarters weren't enough time enclosed. And they hadn't even had the decency to tell him what he'd done! They just pointed their energy rifles at him, told him (oh, most politely) to "Walk this way, sir," and led him here.

And they'd locked him into his cell, leaving him to curse the walls, and scream his anger and frustration at guards who might have been deaf.

The door suddenly rattled. Bill Wagner was on his feet in a second, moving forward. *Finally*! he told himself. *When I find Simmons, I'll wring his neck!*

But it was Felix Alonzo who pushed the door open. Wagner froze. On the floor outside lay a guard, a pool of blood slowly spreading around him.

Wagner looked at the body, then at the pair of energy pistols Alonzo held. "What do you think you're doing?" he demanded.

Alonzo tossed him one of the pistols. "We're leaving," he said. "It's all blown up in our faces. They know we're the ones who stole the artifacts, and they know we're the ones smuggling drugs to the miners. We've got to get off-planet *now*!"

Wagner pushed his way into the hall. The door to the next cell stood open; Clay lay inside, a startled expression on his face. A hole had been burned through the center of his forehead.

Alonzo scarcely gave the corpses a glance, though. He started down the hallway, and Wagner fell into step behind him. When they reached the front door, Wagner noted two more guards slumped over their desks. One had managed to get his stungun out, but hadn't managed to fire before Alonzo burned him down.

Wagner caught Alonzo's arm. "What's going on outside?" he demanded. "Are the shuttles being guarded?"

"If they are, we'll kill the guards and take one anyway."

"The *Constellation*'s drives aren't aligned yet, but they'll do to get us out of orbit. I can fix them myself. There are places I know where the ship can be sold . . . so once you get me into orbit, it won't be hard for me to get away."

"Us," Alonzo said. "I'm going with you."

"Why?"

"Take a look! They'll think you shot your way out of the cell, but they still know enough about me to drag me into this. If I thought I could stay and get away with it, I would. But it's too late. Besides, you owe me now—I got you out. And I have money, and friends who can get us new identities."

"I have the same friends," Wagner said. "And I have more money than I'll spend in ten lifetimes."

"I'll kill you if you don't," Alonzo said, perfectly serious.

Wagner paused only a second. "For old time's sake," he said, and cracked a smile. "But hurry. It won't take them long to find the dead guards."

Alonzo grinned. "We'll be gone by then."

A large jumpcar landed between two of the storage sheds, bringing a pause to the celebration. It was Carter Simmons who climbed out, though. Zeke went forward to see what news he had.

The planetary supervisor was grim. "Someone—I assume it was Alonzo—killed four guards at the detention building, then murdered Clay and freed Wagner. They're loose somewhere."

Zeke found his mouth suddenly dry. "And your men—?"

"I've got everyone I could find armed and out looking for them. There's no telling what they're going to do. I've just sent extra men to guard the shuttles in case they head there, but I'm more worried that they'll try to kill you."

"I don't think you have to worry about it," Jackson said, pointing. "Look."

They turned to follow his finger. And there, bright against the cloud cover, they saw a flaring light: the glow from a shuttle's thrusters.

"The *Constellation*—" Zeke said.

Simmons shook his head. "It's not going anywhere. Remember when you told me to make up an excuse to have my techs continue their work? I had them disassemble the drive system. It would take one man working alone several weeks to get it reassembled and running properly."

"Then they've just trapped themselves," Jackson said.

"That's right," Simmons said. "I'll send men up to get them tomorrow. It shouldn't be too hard to get them to cooperate. There's not much you can do in a driveless hulk."

Felix Alonzo watched Komako shrink from an endless ocean of clouds to a small gray disk, feeling curiously drained. It had been a long emotional high, he thought; sending Clay to kill Bones, freeing Wagner, stealing the shuttle . . . but at least his gamble had paid off. They were free, and they had a ship with a fortune in its holds. Nothing could stop them now.

He was feeling so happy he even answered Simmons's radio call. He jabbed the button and sneered as the vidiscreen filled with Simmons's face.

"What do you want?" he demanded.

"I order you to return here at once."

At that, he had to laugh. "So you can lock me up? Then ship me out for the company's legal department to kick around? No thank you."

"The *Constellation*'s drive isn't working."

"Wagner can fix it."

"Not before we get up there. You'll make things much easier for us if you give yourselves up . . . I'll make a note of that in my report."

Alonzo laughed at him, and flicked off the vidiscreen. *Fool*, he thought.

He went forward to watch the shuttle dock with the *Constellation*—a sight that always impressed him, no matter how many times he saw it.

"He's determined not to make it easy for us," the last Knight said.

He glanced over at his King.

"Do you blame him?" Bones asked. "What do they have to lose at this point?"

"Nothing, I guess. I'll start gathering my men. They can go up in the robodrones. It's not the most comfortable transport, but it'll do."

"You're welcome to use my shuttle."

"That will make things infinitely easier—and faster."

"Any time," the King said, smiling his blessing. "I'm just glad to get this whole mess finally sorted out."

Aboard the *Constellation*, Felix Alonzo was cursing and feeling sick. He was used to starships in acceleration, providing a simulated gravity, but here he floated in zero gee. His stomach kept trying to heave, and it wasn't a pleasant sensation.

And to make things worse, the place stank of sweat and piss and mold and everything else unpleasant he could think of. It was a thoroughly nauseating reek. If they didn't get moving soon, he knew he was going to be sick.

"Hurry up with that!" he demanded.

"For the thousandth time, *no!*" Wagner said. "You can't rush the power-up, or anything else, if you want to do a good job!" He had begun starting the nuclear reactor only twenty minutes before, but it seemed to be taking forever.

Alonzo growled to himself. Somehow, he managed to keep quiet, and then the silence stretched endlessly around him. He found himself acutely aware of the cabin's every smell. *God, this place stinks,* he thought. He tried to focus his attention on something else.

Wagner started going through pre-flight diagnostics. Alonzo floated over and watched in silence.

And suddenly a block of alarm lights began flashing red. Wagner began to curse.

"What is it?" Alonzo said.

"Someone disassembled the shielding around the main thrusters. We're not going anywhere."

"Why? Can't you start them anyway?"

"The engines might work for a time—a short time—before everything ran too hot. But I'm not sure. I've never done it before, and I'm not going to start now. For all I know, it could wreck the engines completely."

"How long will it take to fix?"

"Days, maybe weeks."

Alonzo gestured at the controls. "Just get us out of orbit. That's all I want. When we're away from the planet you can worry about fixing stuff."

"No," Wagner said stubbornly. "I don't work that way. If the ship doesn't check out one hundred percent, we're not going anywhere."

"They'll be up here soon!"

Wagner shrugged. "It's better to be safe."

"It's better to be *free*!"

"It's better to be alive."

"Stupid *bastard*!" Alonzo roared. "I killed five people to get you up here! You said it would work without the shielding! Now *get the goddamn ship moving*!"

"No," Wagner said, folding his arms across his chest.

Alonzo slugged him with the barrel of the energy pistol. Droplets of blood flew from the cut his blow opened on Wagner's forehead, and Wagner himself went glassy eyed.

"I don't need you," Alonzo sneered. "These things are so automated *anyone* can run them!"

He pushed Wagner's body away from the controls, then flicked on the computer. It answered him instantly.

"Plot course toward black hole station," he said.

"Laid in," the computer said a fraction of a second later.

"Prepare to fire main engines."

"Warning—shielding is down. Firing the engines at this time may cause serious harm to the ship and its occupants—"

"Override," Alonzo said.

"Second warning—"

"*Override!*"

". . . done."

"Fire the engines."

He felt the rumble of the acceleration starting. The ship began to move, lending the universe direction again and pushing him toward the floor. He settled into an acceleration couch.

He looked at Wagner, who now lay on the floor, bleeding heavily from the cut on his forehead. "See?" he said. "I told you so—"

Red lights began flashing on the control panel. He spun to look, panicked. For a moment he saw something brighter than anything he'd ever seen before—

In space, a new star flared for an instant, its light intense as a miniature nova. A second later it faded, then was gone.

Chapter Seventeen

Dr. Ezekiel Bones watched the *Constellation*'s engines overheat and explode for the fifth time that afternoon. He winced as the pilot's cabin and everything in it vanished in a flash, then reappeared, blackened, twisted—dead.

Harry and Cal had beamed down the *Ostrum's* recording of what had happened to the freighter an hour before. Zeke couldn't help but feel sick at the thought of all that had been wasted aboard her—not only Wagner's and Alonzo's lives, and the lives of the men they'd killed, but the freighter itself, and all the time and effort they'd spent in tracking down the stolen artifacts.

He sighed unhappily. *At least it's over now.*

Luckily, the cargo bays, floating out behind, hadn't been affected. They floated like a string of squared-off pearls in perfect orbit. The next ore freighter through the system would pick them up and carry them on to the company's base.

He rewound the tape and started to play it again, but Reelys reached out one green tendril and forced his hand back.

"No, Zeke," the shri said. "You have better things to do than watch morbid scenes over and over again."

"I keep thinking it's somehow my fault. If I'd done something different, or said something to them, maybe they wouldn't be dead now . . . maybe nobody would be dead."

Reelys just floated there for a long minute. Finally s/he said, "Ezekiel, you cannot be personally responsible for the actions of strangers. Particularly when those strangers are acting against the interests and customs of their society. They *were* criminals in every sense of the word."

"I suppose you're right," he said. "But I don't have to feel good about it."

"Death is a natural process. But you are right, no being should feel too comfortable with it. It is never a topic to be taken lightly."

"And I think it's time for us to go back to Earth. I no longer feel right about this excavation. I'm sure it should be continued—I think there's still much to be learned from the saurian culture, particularly if they were advanced enough to be using genetic manipulation—but I don't think I'd feel comfortable doing the work myself."

"The artifacts in the freighter's cargo hold can be carried on to Griynsh for the Galactic Museum to study. With all the information you gathered, I do not doubt that they will send a new research team."

Zeke sighed again. "So that's it," he said. "The end of our excavation here."

"No, Ezekiel—it's the beginning of a larger excavation. One must always look to the future. I find it one of humanity's most refreshing traits."

At that Zeke laughed. "You continue to amaze me," he said, standing. "Well, let's not dawdle. I'm sure the others will want to hear. We can start wrapping things up tomorrow, and we can leave two days after that."

Everything from the worktables to the storage sheds had to be dismantled and packed up, then stowed away on the *Heinrich Schliemann*. They had to put away the few artifacts still out, label everything, and send it up to the cargo holds, along with copies of the excavation's notes and records, and all the detailed catalogs and sketches and vids they'd made. Future scholars would need them to carry on the work.

The last day on Komako was perhaps the most hectic of all. While Marty and Jackson handled the final few details of the shuttle, and Siona roamed the miners' camp with Reelys and Sylvie (filming, Zeke gathered, last-minute interviews and statements for the documentary she was putting together), Zeke found himself in the planetary supervisor's office filling out reports.

"Now the criminal activities reports for the murders," Simmons said, and handed him a centimeters-thick stack of papers to look through.

Fortunately, Zeke realized, Simmons had already done the bulk of the work. But what the planetary supervisor seemed to want most was for him to initial the reports as well—to lend the Bones name to them, as if that would somehow remove all the stains from what had happened on Komako.

So he sighed, and he read, and he signed where appropriate. He admired Simmons's ideals, and the way he'd set up the camp and mining pits, and he wanted to encourage that, rather than stifle it. That alone made him willing to put up with more than usual in terms of bureaucracy.

As Komakoans calculated time, it was early evening when the *Heinrich Schliemann* finally lifted off. The trip to the *Ostrum* was uneventful—pleasantly so, Zeke thought. He'd actually begun looking forward to arriving home.

He glanced to the back of the cabin, where Siona and Marty were snuggling together and giggling like children. *I never thought it would last so long,* he thought, glad somehow that it had.

"Didn't I tell you she was perfect for him?" Sylvie asked.

"Hmm?" Zeke blushed; his thoughts had been transparent. "I think you did. And I also remember you telling me you didn't trust her."

"I was wrong, I admit it. She's really a wonderful person. Very sweet."

"Don't let Reelys hear you talking like that—you'll lose your tough reporter image!"

She laughed and patted the holocam beside her. "Never, Zeke."

"We're ready to dock," Jackson called back.

"Let's go forward and watch," Sylvie suggested.

"A romantic thought," Zeke said, and winked.

Hand in hand, he and Sylvie went forward to watch the shuttle match spin and dock with the *Ostrum*. *Two can play at Siona's game of romance,* he thought.

Cal and Harry had the trip back planned and running on a tight schedule. They were at the airlocks to greet Zeke and his friends, and as soon as everyone had come aboard, they hurried off to prepare the hibernation chambers.

Zeke laughed. "Can't wait to get the machinery running," he said. "That's the price of working with technophiles."

"It's time to eat," Marty announced. "Any chance of a late supper, Doc?"

"Sounds good to me," Zeke said. "Why don't you fix it?"

"Great," Jackson said. "He's at his best programming the autochef for hlidskji home cooking."

"Okay, so I made one mistake!" Marty said. "It didn't taste that bad."

"It tasted like mud soup," Sylvie said. "Ugh!"

"If you can do better—" Marty started.

"A !xaka! could do better!" Jackson said. "Why don't you let Sylvie and me handle supper? It's a matter of self-preservation."

"Come on, Siona," Marty said. "You can give me a hand fixing *our* food."

"I'd love to," she said, "but I was hoping Zeke would give me a tour of the ship. We rushed in here at Earth, and I've never seen a ship like this before—"

Zeke grinned and offered her his arm. "I'd be glad to," he said.

The *Ostrum*, despite its size, didn't have that much of note; it had originally been outfitted for a large crew, but equipment now occupied much of the free space. First he led her through the galley, then the biological study room, with its complete medical facilities. Then he took her to the central control room, the true heart of the ship.

It was a large room, with huge vidiscreens showing views of the stars and the planet below from various points on the ship. The computer that controlled navigation and the Invariance Overdrive on their long journeys seemed almost insignificantly small. It took up only a small corner of one wall.

Zeke took it all in with one magnificent sweep of his arm. "Everything is run from here," he said. "Without the computer, we'd be months of subjective time, and years of realtime, in getting back to Earth."

"Oh," Siona said. "That's really what I wanted to know."

"I'm afraid that's it. There's really not that much more to see." He sniffed and smelled something like ham coming from the direction of the galley. Grinning, he said, "Let's get back. I think supper's done." He started for the door.

"Not so fast," Siona said.

"What?" Zeke turned around—and found Siona holding an energy pistol leveled at his stomach. He tensed.

"Don't move," Siona said. "I can burn you where you stand before you take two steps."

"I don't understand," he said slowly. "Why are you doing this?"

"Believe me, Zeke, I don't want to. But I'm a *spy*. I make my living stealing one company's secrets for its competition. When I was hired to accompany you, I thought it was just going to be a routine assignment—get close to Marty, find out what he knows, tell my bosses. End of story.

"But it's not that simple. After I'd signed the contract, they psychoscreened me. I'm sorry, Zeke—I'm supposed to make sure you don't come back in a hurry."

She raised her pistol. Zeke tensed, heart pounding, adrenaline surging as he prepared to jump for cover, though he knew he'd never make it—

Then Siona turned the pistol and fired it point-blank into the navigation computer. Flames crackled and snapped behind the control; an alarm began to scream somewhere overhead. Siona fired again, and again. Plastic caught fire, sending up roiling clouds of smoke.

Zeke chose that second to act. He sprang forward and knocked the pistol from Siona's hand.

She didn't try to stop him. As the fire extinguishers in the computer automatically put out the blaze, she covered her face with her hands and began to cry.

Zeke picked up the energy pistol grimly. "Who hired you?" he demanded.

"I—I don't know—" she sobbed. "It was all—done through middlemen—"

Footsteps pounded down the corridor outside, and a second later Marty and Jackson appeared in the doorway. After them came Cal and Harry. Sylvie and Reelys brought up the rear.

Marty took in the scene in a second and rushed toward Siona, but Zeke grabbed his arm and held him back. "She was sent to kill me," he said, indicating the energy pistol.

"No—"

"Yes," Siona said through her tears. "It was a job, Marty. That's all."

Zeke said, "But she couldn't do it. So she decided to carry out her instructions to the letter—make sure I didn't get back by destroying the *Ostrum's* navigation system."

"Siona—" Marty said. There was raw pain in his voice, love betrayed.

"I'm sorry," she whispered.

Still holding the energy pistol, Zeke took Siona's arm and helped her to her feet. "Come on," he said. "Jackson, give me a hand."

Jackson took her other arm, and together they propelled her out into the corridor. Zeke turned left, heading for the center of the ship.

"Put her in deepsleep?" Jackson asked.

Zeke nodded. "Until we get back to Earth."

Siona made no protest. They quickly prepared her for the hibernation chamber, and she climbed into the coffinlike box without a protest. The lid closed and the inside began to fill with its glowing yellow gasses.

Marty had followed them. He stood in the doorway and watched until Siona's face couldn't be seen anymore.

Finally done, Zeke turned to the hlidskji. He met his friend's accusing stare without protest or apology.

"There's not much more to do," Jackson said behind him.

"I was going to ask her to marry me when we got back to Earth," Marty said.

"I'm sorry," Zeke said.

"But it was all an act."

"I don't think so," he said. "She cared about us enough that she couldn't just kill me, like she was supposed to. We meant something to her. You became more than just a job."

"I suppose."

"Like they say in the Legion," Zeke said, "you've got to keep working if you're going to try to forget. Give me a hand digging the spare navigation computer from ship's stores?" He silently gave thanks that he took precautions and was always prepared for accidents—and sabotage.

"Sure," Marty said numbly. He followed Zeke into the hall. "What's going to happen to her?"

"We'll discuss that later, when we get back to Earth. She was psychoscreened, ordered to do something she normally wouldn't have even considered. And she didn't succeed. I imagine she'll be deported to her home world, and that will be the end of it."

"I'm glad," Marty said. "She really did mean well. I believe that."

"Me, too," Zeke said. He put his arm around his friend's shoulder. "Me, too."

"Sure, Zeke." But somehow, Marty didn't sound convinced.

Visual Data by
Joel Hagen

Beta Caloris IV was an ideal site to the Panadium
Trading and Mining Company (subsidiary of BEC) for
the extraction of minerals and ore. And Carter Simmons,
Planetary Supervisor for Mining Operations, had made
the most of it. The air was strange-tasting but breathe-
able, and although the native vegetation proved inedible,
the soil was non-toxic and supported terrestrial crops.
The miners were well treated and enjoyed the non-
threatening environment—far different from many standard mining worlds.

Orbital mapping suggested several vast areas for exploita-
tion by both open-pit mining and subterranean tunneling.
Carter Simmons's systematic approach and methods for extraction was a high-profit, high-stability affair . . . until the
strange saurian artifacts were discovered.

Closing operations in the highly productive first pit
was frustrating to Simmons, but the BEC directive on
archeological discoveries was quite specific, and Zeke
Bones was as pleased with the unforced compliance as he
was with the artifacts.

The weapons and statues recovered by Simmons's crew
revealed an ancient race that seemed to bear a

remarkable similarity to terrestrial saurians. An intriguing thought, but one which Bones discounted as merely reflecting a lack of detailed information.

When dead miners were found to have been killed with the ancient weapons, rumors of "living dragons" flooded through the miners' camp. To Bones, however, the work was clearly a deadly ruse. The culprit turned out to be Simmons's right-hand man, Alonzo, who was also a drug-and-antiquities smuggler. Bones provided conclusive proof that the saurians were long gone—victims of an artificial virus that had wiped out the majority of the planet's flora and fauna. A virus—Zeke speculated—that might have been synthesized by the saurians themselves and then got out of hand. Its purpose remains a mystery . . . to be solved by the next archeological expedition.

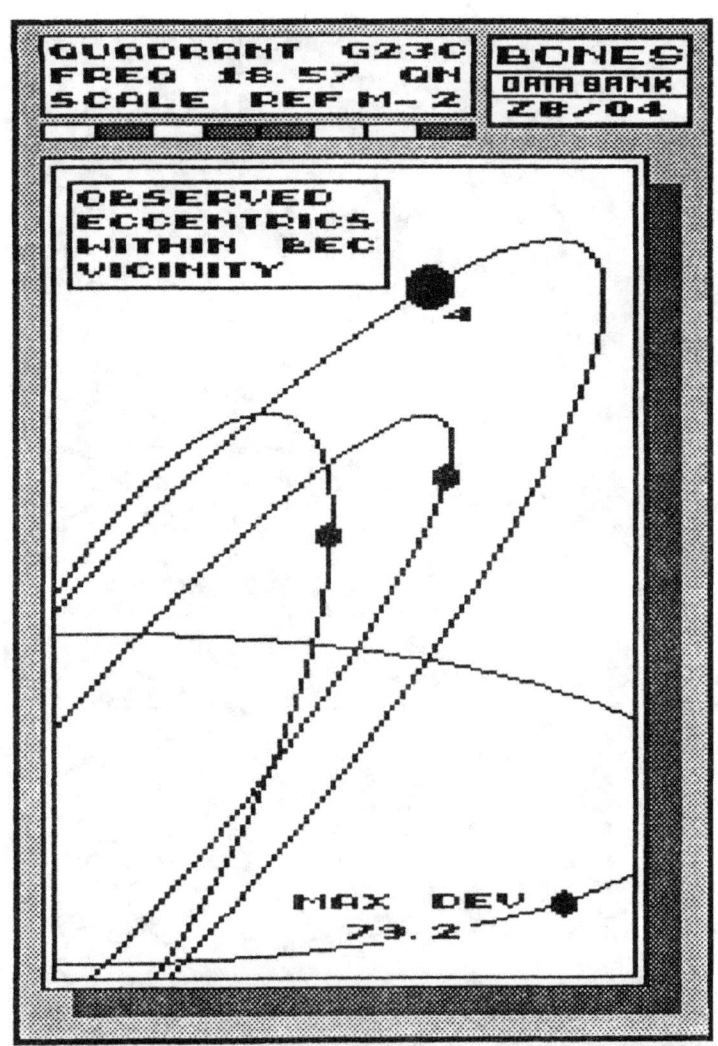

QUADRANT G23C
FREQ 18.57 QM
SCALE REF M-2

BONES
DATA BANK
ZB/04

OBSERVED
ECCENTRICS
WITHIN BEC
VICINITY

MAX DEV
79.2

IMAGING SCREEN   BONES
BETA CALORIS SYSTEM

TARGET SECTOR
1138.95 G2-74
PANADIUM PERM
MINING OPS 3-1

BC-4
NAVCOM LINK

BONES
DATA BANK
ZB/04

IMAGING SCREEN | BONES
BETA CALORIS 4

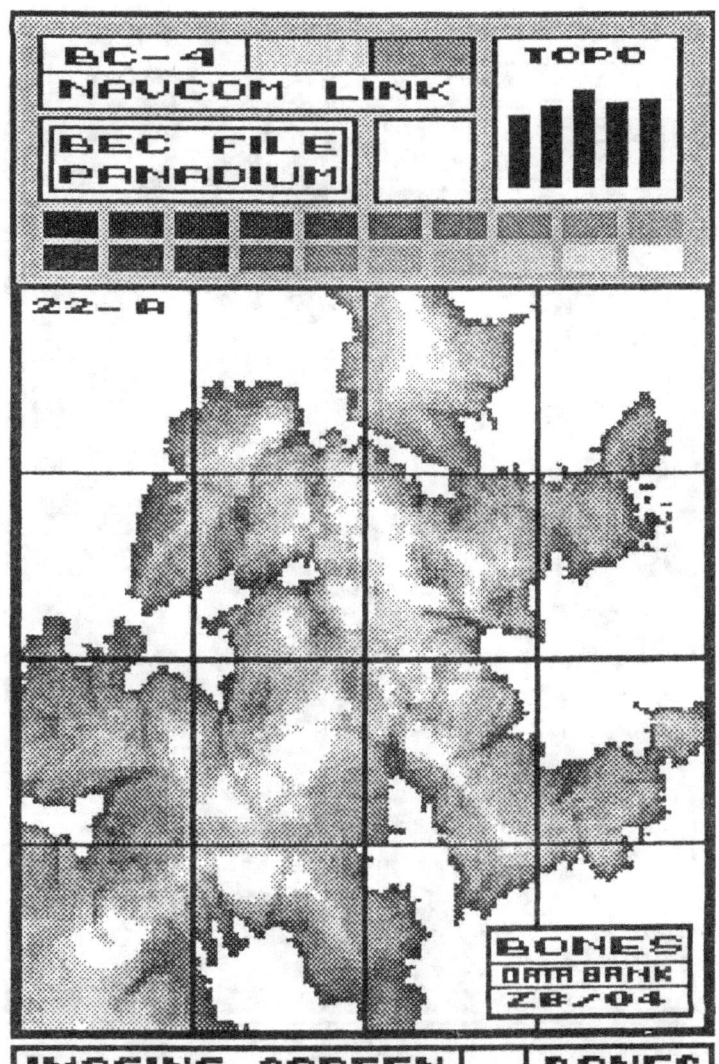

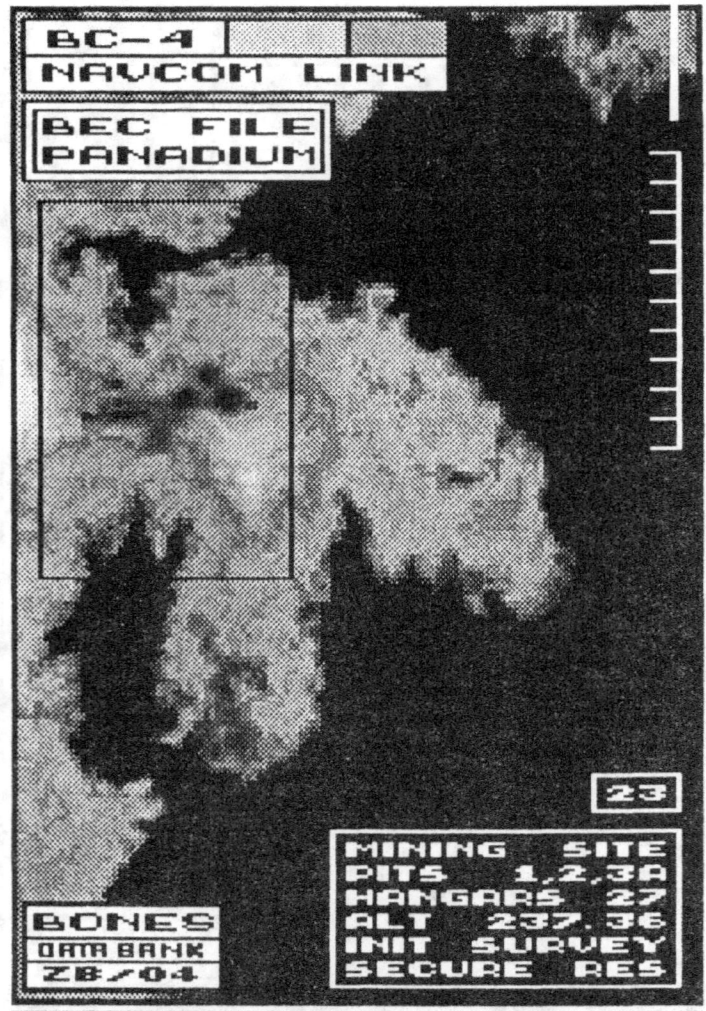

BC-4
NAVCOM LINK

BEC FILE
PANADIUM

23

MINING SITE
PITS 1,2,3A
HANGARS 27
ALT 237.36
INIT SURVEY
SECURE RES

BONES
DATA BANK
ZB/04

IMAGING SCREEN | BONES
AERIAL VIEW PANAD 23

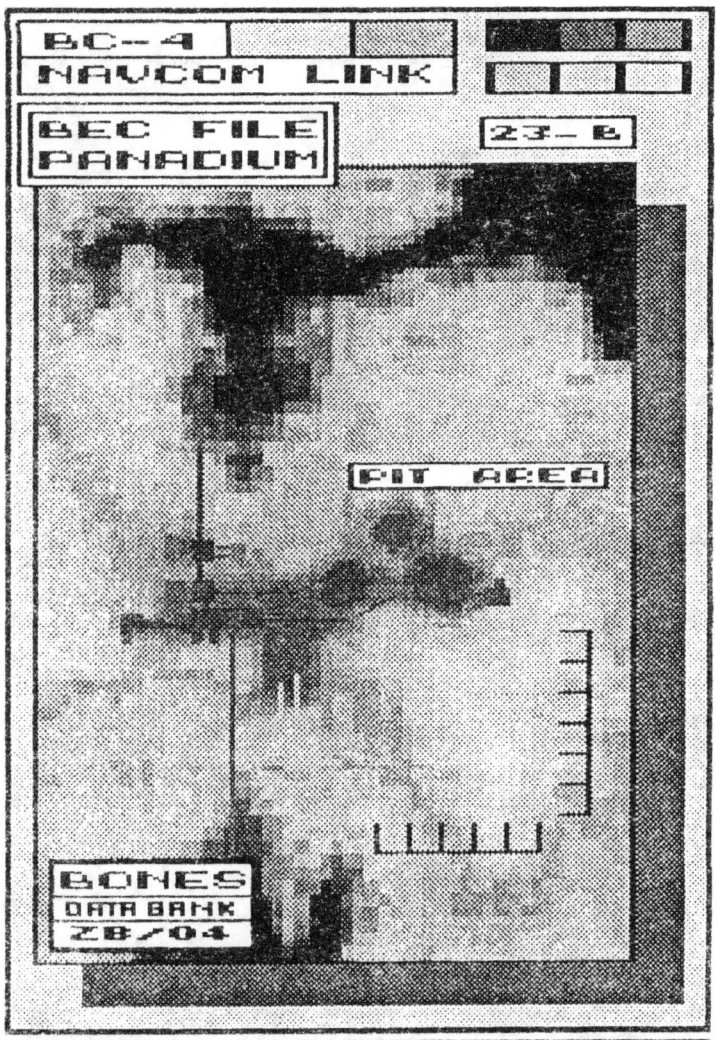

BC--4
NAVCOM LINK

BEC FILE
PANADIUM

23-B

PIT AREA

BONES
DATA BANK
ZB/04

IMAGING SCREEN | BONES
AERIAL ENLARGEMENT

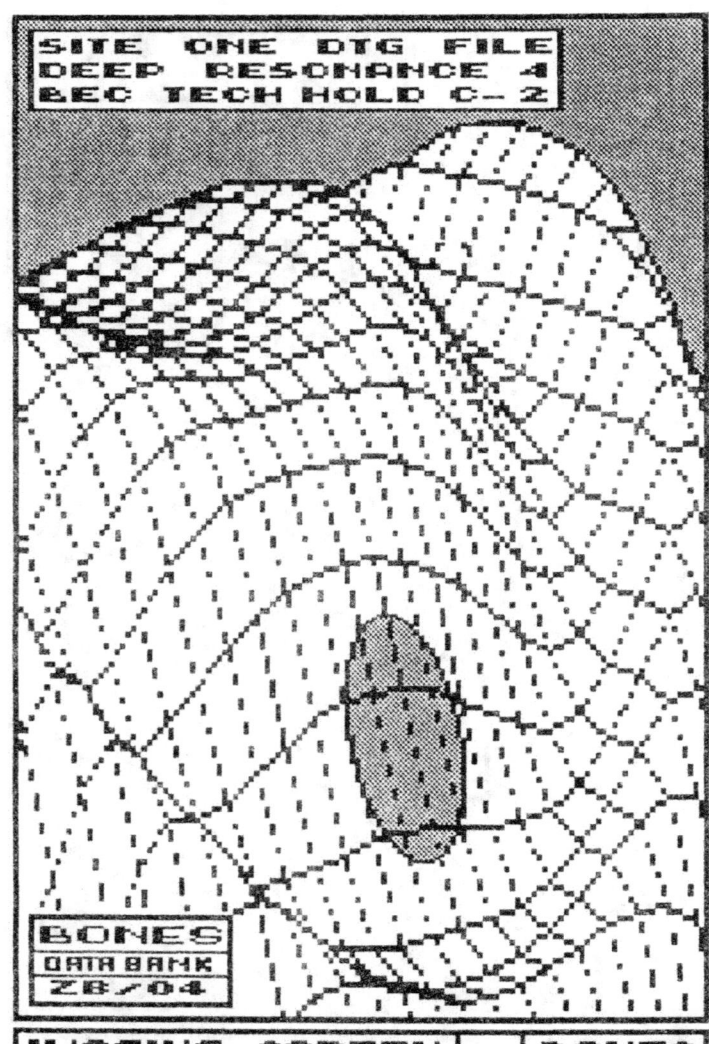

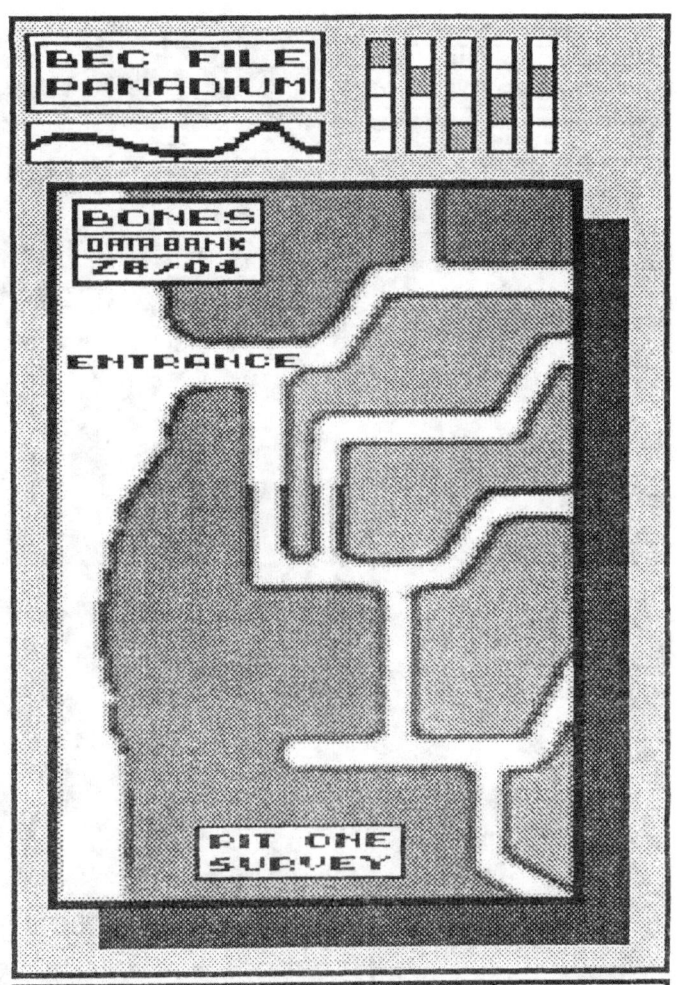

BEC FILE
PANADIUM

BONES
DATA BANK
ZB/04

ENTRANCE

PIT ONE
SURVEY

| IMAGING SCREEN | | BONES |
| TUNNEL PLAN VIEW | |

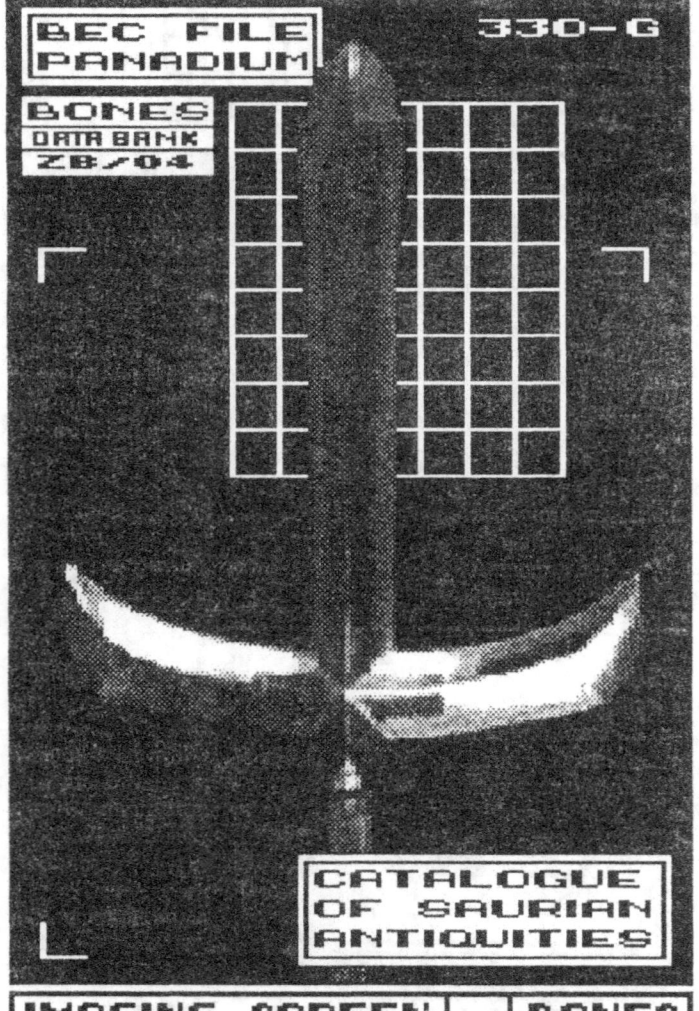

BEC FILE
PANADIUM

330-G

BONES
DATA BANK
ZB/04

CATALOGUE
OF SAURIAN
ANTIQUITIES

IMAGING SCREEN | BONES
SAURIAN SPEAR

CATALOGUE
OF SAURIAN
ANTIQUITIES

| 1 | 2 | 3 | 4 |
| 5 | 6 | 7 | 8 |

REF. 0721
BC-4 ZOO

BONES
DATA BANK
ZB/04

| IMAGING SCREEN | BONES |
| DIGIT STRUCTURE | |

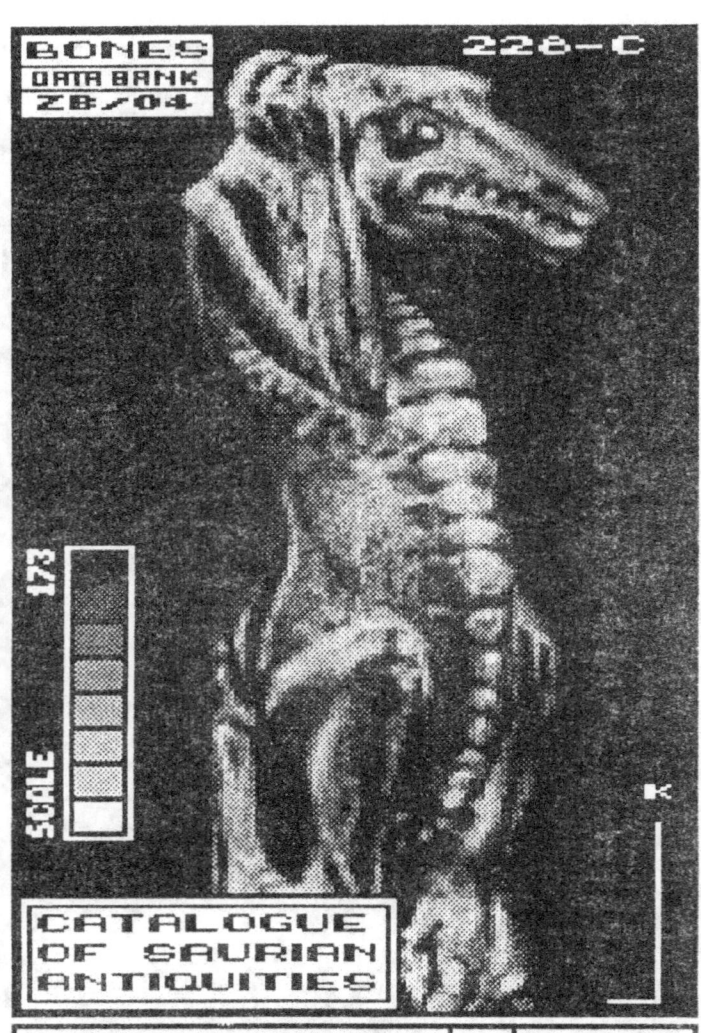

BONES
DATA BANK
ZB/04

228-C

173

SCALE

CATALOGUE
OF SAURIAN
ANTIQUITIES

K

IMAGING SCREEN   BONES
DRAGON SCULPTURE

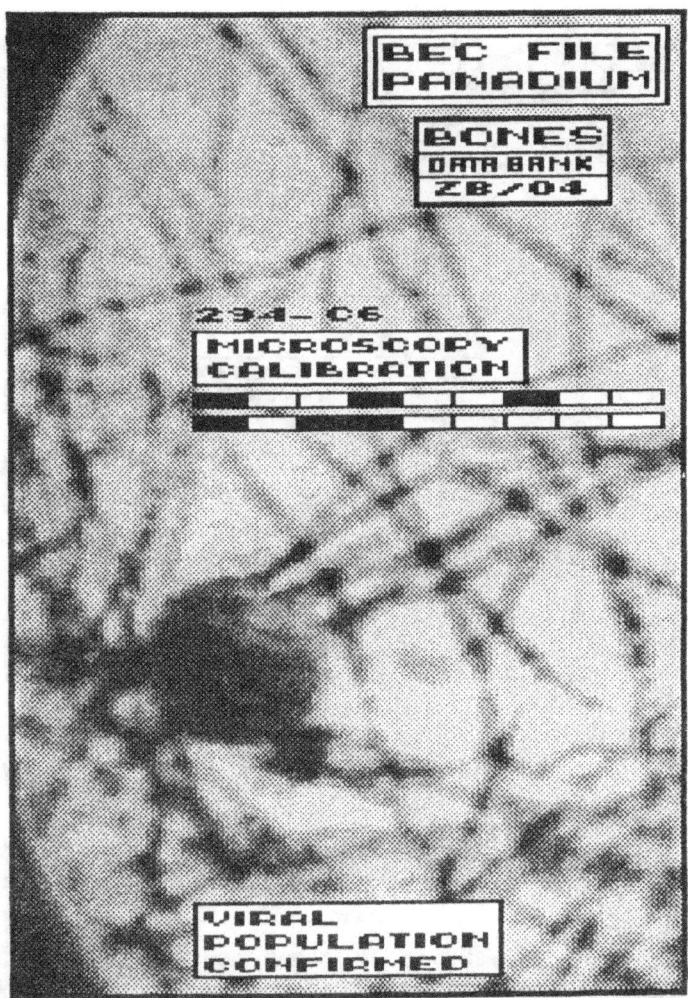

BEC FILE
PANADIUM

BONES
DATA BANK
ZB/04

234- C6

MICROSCOPY
CALIBRATION

VIRAL
POPULATION
CONFIRMED

IMAGING SCREEN   BONES
VIRUS IN GRASS SAMPLE

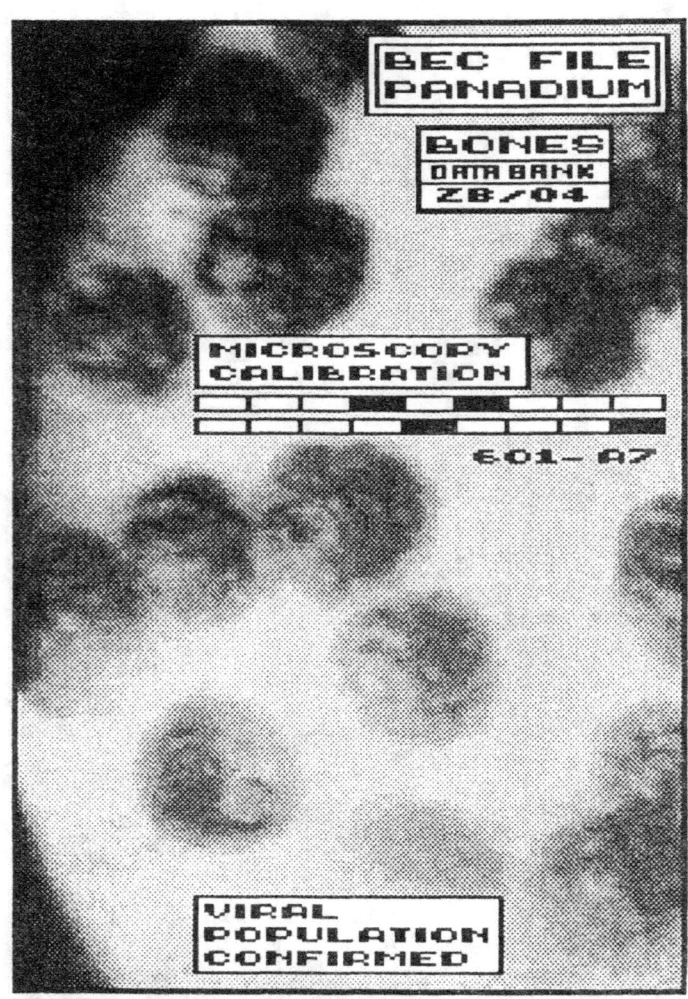

BEC FILE
PANADIUM

BONES
DATA BANK
ZB/04

MICROSCOPY
CALIBRATION

6.01 - A7

VIRAL
POPULATION
CONFIRMED

IMAGING SCREEN | BONES
VIRUS IN FISH SAMPLE